MOCHITA STAGE

e Sherman is puzzled by the identity of strange riders who pass him on their into Blundell. But it's not long before thing is sure; they are not around for th reasons and are, in fact, out to join Marsh, the desperado in control of just it everything in town. Could be that a re-coach carrying a handsome load of ey, and a herd of 3000, both due any have something to do with the way dangerous men grow nervous and trigger-happy – and some plain careless.

MOCHITA STAGE

MOCHITA STAGE

by

Hal Jons

Dales Large Print Books
Long Preston, North Yorkshire,
BD23 4ND, England.

British Library Cataloguing in Publication Data.

Jons, Hal
    Mochita stage.

    A catalogue record of this book is
    available from the British Library

    ISBN   978-1-84262-889-8 pbk

First published in Great Britain in 1964 by
Frederick Muller Ltd.

Copyright © 1964 by Hal Jons

Cover illustration © Michael Thomas

The moral right of the author has been asserted

Published in Large Print 2012 by arrangement with
Hal Jons, care of Mrs M. Kneller

Dales Large Print is an imprint of Library Magna Books Ltd.

Printed and bound in Great Britain by
T.J. (International) Ltd., Cornwall, PL28 8RW

CHAPTER ONE

Nobody noticed the dust-covered horse and rider come into town from off the North trail. The crowd were gathered in a ring just outside the saloon with the sign 'Maxims' hanging above its batwing doors. Plenty of dust clouded up from the centre of the ring and out of curiosity Steve Sherman edged his big pinto to the fringe of the crowd.

His features hardened as he took in the scene. A big-chested, black-whiskered man was beating blazes out of a lad who could not have been more than sixteen years of age. The boy was lightly built and although blood poured from a dozen places on his face, his eyes held no fear.

As Steve watched, the boy went down from a sledge-hammer blow to the temple. He tried to rise but his arms gave way and he slumped forward again into the dust. A middle-aged woman in the crowd cried out but was restrained from rushing forward by a couple of younger women. Some of the men in the inside ring yelled encouragement to the big fellow to finish off the job.

'Kick his blamed head in Matt! Get it finished! It's too durned hot out here.' The speaker was a long agile-looking cowboy with a mean look in his pale blue eyes.

Matt spread his lips in a snarl of victory and raised his foot, then turned to look around in amazement as Steve Sherman's voice snapped above the general hubbub.

'Lay off, you polecat! Step back or you're a dead man!'

The crowd turned and followed Matt's surprise gaze. They saw a horse and rider covered in alkali, the horse bigger than average and the man tall in the saddle, slim but wide-shouldered, with fire crackling out of eyes almost hidden in deep sockets. His hands rested quietly on the saddle pommel.

The ring of onlookers broke, leaving a clear channel between the newcomer and Matt Brasher who advanced slowly upon the horseman. Brasher stopped a yard or so from the pinto and glared up at the newcomer.

'You're mighty free with your tongue, Mister,' he said. 'Climb down off'n that cayuse and back up the talk.'

Without a word Steve Sherman swung out of the saddle but before he could reach the ground Brasher rushed forward in an attempt to get him off balance. Steve, sensing the move, swung the pinto around bringing its hindquarters heavily into contact with the man's bulk. Brasher staggered then spread his length in the dust. When he scrambled up Steve was right beside him, and a short crisp right-cross to the throat sent him back to the ground with a thud. Brasher rolled and scrabbled for his gun but as quick as light Steve leapt to his side and rapped him smartly on the side of the head with a gun barrel.

As Brasher lost interest in things his cronies decided to take a hand. Steve swivelled on the balls of his feet and fired once, the bullet sending the gun spinning out of the hand of the lean, mean-looking puncher to the sidewalk. The man and a few others who had their hands on their guns fell back wilting before the fire in Steve's eyes.

The boy pulled himself out of the dust and stood shakily for a minute before crossing to the woman who had cried out. Putting his arm around her shoulders he consoled her and then turned to face Steve.

'Thank you, Mister,' he said simply. 'It's mighty good of you to take sides but you'll need to watch these polecats now that you've crossed 'em. The whole blamed outfit would as soon shoot a man in the back as face to face.'

Steve Sherman nodded and looked around the crowd, fastening his gaze on a wide-shouldered, evil-faced man who toted a star on his vest.

'You the law?' he asked.

The man stared back at him insolently and moved out a bit towards him.

'Yeah. The name's Hart. I'm the Marshal of this township and I'm taking you to the hoosegow. You just broke one of the laws; namely, shooting off that iron of yours.'

The lawman's eyes wavered a bit under Steve's scrutiny as the newcomer moved up close to him.

'Call yourself a lawman,' Steve gritted, holstering his gun. 'What sort of lawman stands by and sees a lad beaten to a pulp by a full grown man?'

'The cheeky young pup asked for what he got,' snarled Hart. 'Accusing Brasher and the rest of his outfit of killing his pa and running off with his stock. If you hadn't horned in Brasher'd have given him a proper lesson as to what he can say to his betters.'

The crowd were getting interested again and Brasher's cronies had the grins back on their faces. It looked as though Marshal Hart was taking the initiative but Steve's next action chilled them. He grabbed for Hart's neck and pulled him into a bone-crushing right hand then he kneed the Marshal viciously in the crutch, sending him into the dust with a shriek of pain.

Slowly Steve took stock of the crowd. Their hands were noticeably well away from their guns. There was plain disgust on his face as he addressed them.

'Get going,' he said quietly. 'Beat it.' And wilting under his air of authority they moved away, some singly, some in groups, until at length only the unconscious Brasher, the groaning Marshal and the boy and his mother remained.

Steve tied his pinto to the hitch-rail and smiled at the woman and boy in a way that transformed his grimed face.

'Thank you Mister,' the woman said in a well-bred voice. 'I'm sure Matt Brasher would have killed Dave if you hadn't come along.'

The boy was wiping away the signs of battle but his eyes were clear and unafraid. Steve warmed to him, liking the spirit that remained unmoved by his near escape.

'Oh, I guess somebody would have horned in before it got that far Ma'am,' Steve replied, removing his Stetson. 'But I reckon Dave would play it smart by keeping outa the way until he's put on a bit more flesh,' he added. 'Sand just ain't enough when tangling with hombres like Brasher.'

A grin edged the youngster's lips but his mother looked serious. 'We'll be moving East pretty soon Mister. I'm hoping Dave will keep clear of trouble until we're on our way. There's nothing left here for us now.'

'The name's Sherman Ma'am, Steve Sherman. Mebbe you'd like to tell me what's been going on. If so, I'll pay you a visit as soon as I leave my mark hereabouts.'

The woman nodded. 'You come to the

11

LazyY Mister Sherman and I'll certainly tell you what's happened these last few months. My name's Pownall,' she added, as she turned to leave. 'Come Dave, drive me home.'

Steve watched the woman and boy cross to a buggy standing outside a store then drive away. Ignoring the two men now sitting up in the roadway, he climbed the sidewalk and pushed into Maxim's saloon. Curious glances followed him as he walked casually to the bar but no one spoke and the two punchers holding up the bar beside him edged away and walked to a table against the wall.

Steve asked the barkeep for rye and without a word the man served him, gave him his change then moved to the far end of the bar. There was a breathlessness about the place as though the occupants were expecting something to happen. He shrugged his shoulders and sipped his drink but his eyes were glued on the big mirror behind the bar that reflected the entire saloon.

The batwing doors swung open and Marshal Hart and Brasher pushed into the saloon. They stood either side of the door, their eyes riveted on Steve's back. The hair started to creep on Steve's scalp as he watched them in the mirror but their hands were well away from their guns. He saw that all heads were turned towards the door as though everybody knew what to expect.

The doors opened again and in strode the long, mean-looking cowboy, a gun in each hand. Steve eased himself away from the bar keeping his eyes on the mirror.

'Hey! You there! Grab your hardware.' Even as the man spoke, he fired but he was too late. Steve saw the guns come into line and like lightning he side-stepped, grabbed for his guns and fired on the turn. The mirror behind the bar smashed into a thousand pieces a split second before the lanky cowboy dropped his guns, clawed at his chest and pitched forward into the sawdust.

'Freeze everybody,' snarled Steve. 'Anybody so much as sneeze and they get lead poisoning.' He motioned with a gun to the customers on one side of the saloon to move over and join the group on the other. They understood readily enough and moved cautiously with their hands held conspicuously away from their six-guns. Brasher and Marshal Hart stepped away from the door and merged with the crowd. Steve walked calmly towards the door. When he came alongside the dead puncher he paused and gave the crowd the full benefit of his fiery gaze.

'This jasper deserved just what he got,' he said tersely. 'Just don't forget how he got his ticket to Boot Hill. I'll be back and anybody with itchy fingers can expect the same medicine.'

Nobody moved until they heard Steve's horse head away up Main Street, then the crowd surged forward to view the corpse and ask each other questions concerning Steve's identity.

Steve set his tired horse in the wake of the Pownall's buggy. The wind was shifting the trail dust quickly but the tracks were still clear enough to make trailing easy.

As he passed the livery stable, two riders passed him on the way into town. Both were big men but the one astride a coal-black gelding impressed him. The man flashed him an all-embracing but disinterested glance and turned in the saddle to say something to his companion. There was the unmistakable stamp of authority in the set of the man's jawline and wide shoulders. His features were clean-shaven and well formed and although his dress was showy, red woollen shirt, pearl-buttoned vest, green silk bandanna and gold piped levis tucked into calf-length 'pee-wee's', he was without doubt a man to be reckoned with.

Steve rode on, shrugging his impressions of the man aside, and gave himself over to following the easy trail the Pownalls' buggy had cut into the dust; but later the man's features reappeared in his mind's eye and there was something vaguely familiar about them which bothered him.

Just two hours later he guided his tired

14

pinto past an empty corral and eased to a halt outside the Lazy Y ranch-house. Dave Pownall came around the ranch building where he had been unhitching the buggy and stabling the horse. He grinned a welcome at Steve and came up to take the pinto.

'I'll see to your bronc Mister Sherman,' he said. 'You go on inside.'

Steve slid out of the saddle, removed his warbag and handed the lead rein over to the boy.

'Thanks,' he replied with a smile. 'No need to call me Mister. The name's Steve.'

'Right, Steve it is.' Dave started to lead the pinto away then turned to yell: 'Hey Mom! We've got company.'

Steve dusted himself down with his Stetson until most of the alkali was removed from his clothes and when he looked up Mrs Pownall was framed in the doorway.

'Come right on in Mister Sherman,' she said. 'I'll have a meal ready just as soon as you've sluiced down.'

Steve stepped up on the verandah and followed her into the ranch-house. He paused at the threshold and admired the room before stepping inside. Every surface gleamed and glistened, a deep Navajo rug covered the entire floor space and big leather armchairs were grouped cosily around an enormous fireplace that housed big wrought-iron ornamented dogs. There was a plentiful supply of brasswork and glassware on the redwood dresser that ranged along one wall, and the covers draped over each chair and the long settle were pristine white.

Mrs Pownall's gaze took in Steve's admiration of the room and her brows furrowed as the distasteful thought of having to leave the home she loved crowded her mind.

'I'll show you to a room where you can get yourself cleaned up Mister Sherman,' she said remembering her duties as a hostess, and when Steve nodded she preceded him through a couple of smaller rooms to one which faced out on to the feed barn. Here again everything was neat and orderly. A single size bed took up a corner, and a table, chair, chest of drawers, wardrobe and washstand made up the rest of the furniture.

Steve set his warbag down on the chair and gazed around appreciatively as Mrs Pownall checked the water in the big china jug that stood in the bowl on the washstand.

'I guess you'll manage to get cleaned up,' she said. 'I'll get Dave to change the water afterwards.'

'It's mighty good of you, Ma'am,' Steve replied. 'Although I sure hope I'm not being a nuisance.'

She stood at the doorway looking back at him and shook her head slowly.

'You're welcome to any hospitality I can provide Mister Sherman. You intervened today to save Dave when a lot of men who used to call themselves friends were standing by. You're welcome to make this your home until we move out.'

Before Steve could answer, she went through the door, closing it behind her. Left to himself he stripped and scrubbed his body free from trail dust. He reflected that the Lazy Y showed no signs of running to seed. The ranch-house and outbuildings were still in good condition. Just the absence of stock all the way through the good graze that stretched from the Blundell trail indicated the end of the Pownall's stay. He had counted no more than fifty head dotted around the wide verdant basin.

Some time later, seated with Dave and Mrs Pownall, enjoying his first home cooked meal in a month, Steve listened to the Pownalls' story, which differed very little from that of all the small ranches around Blundell.

It appeared that a few months ago Abe Marsh had brought a trail herd into the south end of the basin with the alleged intention of grazing them until a herd travelling just ahead was cleared of Texas tick. But he had stayed on, building a ranch-house plumb in the middle of the free graze used by all the small ranchers. From the word go trouble flared up. When it became apparent Marsh was staying, the small ranchers grouped together and demanded that he moved the herd on but Marsh and his roughneck crew made it abundantly clear they were in the basin for keeps. Within the next month fighting broke out whenever Marsh's men came into contact with hands from other spreads and in Blundell they ruled the roost. Marsh himself, a hard-looking but suave operator, moved amongst the troubles unruffled and aloof. Once only had he been prodded to reach for the hardware and Daniel Nover of the Pole Star died before his guns cleared leather. Brasher, Marsh's segundo, a vicious eager gunman, spoiled and prodded at every conceivable opportunity and he had added six notches to his gun since striking the territory.

Loyal hands had died and timid hands had forked their broncs for quieter pastures leaving the small ranchers easy prey. Systematically their stock had been rustled or slaughtered until they were left with nothing worth fighting for except their self-respect.

At the same time Marsh opened a store in Blundell, leaving paid hands to emphasise the folly of using Al Durnett's long-established store. He muscled in on half a dozen gin parlours, the original owners pulling their freight shortly after.

Mog Myers, the Marshal, died in the cross-

18

fire between warring factions in Main Street when two other ranchers died. Marsh's men put up one of their own sidekicks, Clem Hart, for the vacant office and canvassed votes with six-guns at the ready.

Within four months Marsh had Blundell nicely sewn up. Nothing and nobody moved without his say-so. Alec Pownall was the only man left who stood against the newcomer. He died in Blundell trying to take a load of barbed wire from Dunnett's store. Brasher prodded him into going for his guns but Alec died before his hand reached his gunbutts. Doc Haydn told Mrs Pownall later that he had taken three slugs out of her husband's body – two .45s, one .38. The .38 had entered Alec's back. Brasher used Colt .45s.

Doc Haydn wrote later to an old friend, U.S. Marshal Rawlings at Dallas, the letter travelling out of Blundell on the stage-coach run by Tom Digby. Three hold-ups in three months seemed set to put Digby out of business. Up to now Marshal Rawlings had done nothing.

The remainder of the Pownalls' stock disappeared shortly after the last two hands made their apologetic farewells.

Steve listened without interruption until Mrs Pownall had run out of words. He nodded, a grave expression on his face. Words of sympathy would have been inadequate.

'This man Marsh. What does he look like?' he asked after a while.

Between them Mrs Pownall and Dave built up a description that tallied with the impressive looking man Steve had passed just out of town.

'I guess I saw Marsh on my way in,' he said. 'He looks a hombre who'd be mighty hard to remove once he'd decided to stake a claim in the territory.'

'He's surrounded by the toughest crew that ever struck these parts,' put in Dave. 'I guess he's here for keeps and his crew will be gunning for you after what you did to Hart and Brasher.'

The prospect didn't seem to disturb Steve. He pushed his empty plate away with a sigh of satisfaction. He hadn't enjoyed a meal as much for months. Mrs Pownall poured him a mug of steaming coffee and passed it across the table.

'I guess they've got plenty more cause to come gunning now,' Steve said quietly. 'That long cowpoke who was edging Brasher on tried blasting me with his six-guns in the place they call Maxim's. He reckoned without the mirror behind the bar. Anyways, he was plumb out of luck.'

There was respect in Dave's eyes as he flashed a look at Steve. 'That's Ed Millard!' he ejaculated. 'He was some artist with his six-guns.'

Mrs Pownall's face held a worried expression. 'You'd best be moving on Mister Sherman. They won't let up now until they've killed you, and I guess Dave and I had better start out for the East just as soon as we can get our things together.'

'You've got some place to go back East?' asked Steve as he rolled himself a smoke.

Mrs Pownall nodded. 'Yes, I've got a sister in New York. I guess we're lucky. Alec sold a few hundred head to a trail herd just before Marsh struck the territory. That gives us a stake back East. That's not saying we want to go though,' she added. 'The Lazy Y's been my home for a long time. I guess I'll always have a hankering to be back.'

'I'm not promising I won't be back when I reckon I'll stand a chance against these buzzards,' Dave ground out, unable to contain himself any longer. 'I guess there's a lot of range hereabouts that's free to any hombre who elects to stay on it, but there's a strip clear from Lone Wolf Butte to the Red River that my father held title on, and I aim to claim it again at the right time.'

Dave's mouth set in a hard straight line showing the stubborn streak that his father must certainly have possessed, and Steve reckoned that the soft ways of the East would never claim the boy. He would always be hankering for the strip of Texas that was lawfully his.

Steve drew deeply on his cigarette, debating just how much he should say to the Pownalls. He didn't particularly want them to leave for the coast yet he was chary of building up their hopes. It wouldn't be fair to Mrs Pownall anyway to risk Dave's life by persuading them to stay.

'Maybe you'll let me know where I can mail a letter to reach you in New York, Mrs Pownall,' he said at length. 'Next time I ride this way it could be the law's taken things in hand again.'

Mrs Pownall searched for paper and pen, then writing the New York address down passed the paper across the table to Steve. Some of the respect had faded out of Dave's eyes. Steve smiled inwardly as he realised the lad believed the man who had stood against Brasher and Hart was no better than the paid hands who had left when the pace got hot. He drained the last of his coffee and stood up.

'I'll get some shut-eye if you'll excuse me Ma'am,' he said. 'I guess I'll move on at sun-up.'

The Pownalls nodded and watched him go out of the big room.

CHAPTER TWO

Abe Marsh and his constant companion Lew Fallon reined in their mounts and tethered them to the hitchrail outside Maxim's. Together they stepped on to the sidewalk and through the batwing doors. They paused on the threshold and surveyed the ring of men gathered round the dead Ed Millard.

Matt Brasher looked around, and straightening up moved out of line so that his boss could get a good look at the cadaver. Neither Marsh nor Fallon moved a muscle of their faces. Sudden death was part of their stock in trade and they reckoned hired hands were expendable anyway. Their only interest in the event was where it might affect them.

'What happened?' asked Marsh as he searched in his vest pocket for a cheroot.

'Some jasper fresh off the trail horned in when I was giving that Pownall brat a lesson. He swung his cayuse into me an' took Clem Hart by surprise with a humdinger of a punch when Clem made to take him to the chokey.'

Marsh and Fallon listened without interruption. Marsh seemed more interested in getting the end of his cheroot evenly lit whilst Fallon's hooded eyelids slid almost shut as though he was bored with the whole business.

'This buzzard's mighty fast with his shooting irons,' went on Brasher. 'He beat Ed to the draw outside, then later when he was bellied up to the bar an' Ed came in holding his irons, the jasper still outgunned him.'

'Uh-uh,' grunted Fallon. 'Big feller riding a pinto, looks like he's got all the dust of Texas settled on him, that the jasper?'

Brasher nodded. 'Yeah. He hightailed it pronto. Said he'd be back but I don't reckon so.'

Marsh's pale blue eyes rested on Brasher briefly. There was a quality in the glance that had Brasher swallowing hard.

'When that sort of hombre says he'll be back, you can bet your last red cent he'll do just that.' Marsh took a deep pull on his cigar and glanced quickly at Fallon then back to Brasher. The crowd around Millard's body fell away as Fallon walked towards the bar.

'I'd prefer that something stopped this feller from coming back into town,' Marsh said quietly, calmly surveying the end of his cigar, then he followed in Fallon's wake.

Brasher looked round the crowded saloon and motioned two of his sidekicks to follow him then pushed his way out to the sidewalk. When the other two joined him they unhitched their nodding horses and rode out of town towards the Pownalls' spread.

It needed another half an hour to sundown when the three men reined in their mounts on the fringe of a belt of cottonwoods overlooking the Pownall's headquarters.

'His tracks lead down there sure enough,' growled Brasher. 'I reckon he's got his feet under the table by now digging into a man-size meal. There's nothing worse'n a full belly for slowing a man up. You'd better ride around to that clump of junipers Moody. Leave your cayuse there and come into the house the back way. Parry an' me'll give you plenty of time to get inside then keep outa things until we start the music going.'

Moody, a wiry, pock-marked gun slinger, grinned in evil anticipation. He glanced across to the distant junipers.

'Gawd, that's gonna be some walk,' he grumbled, the amusement fading from his face. 'You'd better give me about fifteen minutes after sundown.'

Brasher nodded and as Moody rode away he turned his mount back deep into the cottonwoods. Parry followed and when they judged themselves immune from the danger of being seen, they rolled themselves cigarettes and smoked out the time to sundown.

The two men waited until they judged Moody was well on his way then they rode out of the copse and on down to the ranchhouse. Brasher slid out of the saddle and hitched the lead rein over the hitch-rail. The door opened as he set foot on the bottom step to the veranda and Dave Pownall stood framed in the doorway. The youngster glared down at the hulking gunman, his mouth in a tight line.

'Tell that visitor of yours to show his face. I want to palaver with him pronto,' growled Brasher.

Dave eyed the man sneeringly. 'I'll tell him Brasher,' he said, 'But my guess is he'll do as he pleases.'

As Brasher came up the steps fast to gain a foothold, Dave slammed the door and shot the bolts in place. He turned away from the door to face his mother who had come into the living room.

'It's Brasher and his sidekick Parry Mom,' he said in reply to the question that showed in her eyes. 'They want Steve Sherman. I guess they're wanting to even the scores.'

The colour drained from Mrs Pownall's face. 'Now you keep out of things Dave. You just go and tell Mister Sherman that they're out there, and keep out of the way. There's no sense in getting killed before you've started living.'

Dave shook his head and there was a stubborn look on his face.

'I'll tell him,' he said. 'But I don't reckon on letting him fight our battles without siding him.'

Mrs Pownall went to remonstrate with her son, then biting her lip turned away from him. As Dave went through to Steve's room, she took down the Sharps repeater that rested on a couple of wall brackets. If her son was going to be involved, Ruth Pownall was going to be in it up to the neck.

Steve had just dropped off into the first light dozing sleep when the noise of Brasher's arrival jerked him back to full consciousness. At the sound of Brasher's voice he was out of bed in a flash. Pausing briefly to listen he judged by the shifting restless horses that no more than two riders were outside. He pulled his denims on and strapped his gunbelt around his middle, then crossing to the window he opened it wide enough to climb through. He dropped to the ground between the house and feed barn a split second before Dave opened the door of his room.

Quickly Steve considered the situation. He knew enough about Brasher's sort to realise that the element of surprise would be used. If Brasher and another rider were out front then for his money there'd be some other killer planted at the back. Drawing his left side Colt, he rushed around the building, his hyper-sharp eyes catching sight of Moody's leg before it disappeared through the back window.

Steve was beside the window in a flash. The door separating the back room from the front room opened a crack, letting a slit of light into the back room, then most of the light was shielded by the man who peered through and waited his cue. Brasher was shouting now and threatening to shoot his way in and Steve's lips tightened as he saw how well they had prepared the trap.

He eased himself through the window with an uncanny absence of noise. Instinctively he rounded a table and crept nearer the man at the door. When just a couple of yards separated them, the man's sixth sense got to work. He swung round but Steve's gun butt crashed down on his head. With no more than a gasp he slumped forward and Steve caught him on his way down, letting him gently to the floor.

Holstering his own gun, he reached down and slid the man's weapons out of their holsters. Climbing back out of the window and rounding the house he slipped the guns under the feed barn then carefully edged to the end of the veranda. Enough light filtered through the front curtained window to show Brasher plainly enough but the other horse and rider were just a deeper blue in the gloom.

'I'll give up to five to send that hombre out Pownall,' Brasher shouted. 'Then I'm shooting my way in.'

Steve took a deep breath and eased his guns into his hands. Brasher had got to 'two'.

'I'm right here feller. What's the beef?' yelled Steve then he slid aside like greased lightning as he saw movement on the part of the rider in the shadows. He was only just in time. Two gun flashes stabbed out of the darkness and bullets tore into the veranda rail where he had stood. Steve's answering shot brought a scream of pain and he heard the rider tumble from his horse. Brasher charged into the shadows but made the cardinal error of shooting a stream of bullets in Steve's general direction. One or two winged past too close for comfort but Steve took steady aim, judging Brasher's position from the last flash. He fired and heard Brasher crash to the ground.

At that moment the ranch-house door was flung open spreading light on the scene. After a pause Dave Pownall came through the doorway holding a shotgun.

'I guess the fireworks are finished Dave,' called Steve, making his way towards the two still forms. Dave didn't answer but watched while Steve bent over the two men in turn.

'Both dead,' announced Steve quietly as he stood upright and crossed over to the boy. He caught sight of Mrs Pownall just inside the room, holding a rifle in the way that indicated she'd use it if pressed. He herded Dave inside the house and shut the door.

'You can relax Mrs Pownall,' he said quietly. 'Those hombres aren't gonna trouble anyone again.'

Mrs Pownall dropped the rifle to the rug and passed a nervous hand over her face.

'I guess I'll never be able to thank you enough Mister Sherman,' she said. 'If you hadn't handled things Dave would have tangled with that Brasher again and – and Dave's not ready to deal with men yet.'

Steve smiled, the harsh lines of his face relaxing into good looks.

'My guess is that before long Dave'll handle anything that turns up,' he said.

Dave flashed him a grateful glance. 'I sure was surprised to find your room empty Steve,' he said. 'Things looked mighty awkward to me.'

Steve grinned and crossed to the door leading to the back room which was still slightly ajar. He pushed it open and dragged the still unconscious body of his first victim into the room. Dave and Mrs Pownall watched him in amazement. The respect was back in Dave's eyes as he stared at Steve.

'I opined if Brasher was loud-mouthing out front, he'd planted some insurance at the back,' Steve said simply.

'That's Moody,' put in Dave. 'Always itching to go for his gun. He killed Mike Summers, the Cross Keys boss.'

Steve nodded. 'Got any rye or bourbon?' he asked Mrs Pownall. She came out of her daze and went to a cupboard, bringing out a bottle of rye and some glasses.

Half filling one of the glasses Steve hauled the wiry Moody on to the large settle and forced some of the spirit into the man's mouth. The man gagged on the spirit and at length his eyes flickered open. It was a full minute before reason showed in them, then he stared back at the trio of faces above him. He felt his head gingerly then cocked it to one side as though listening for sounds of help.

'Who sent you, Moody?' Steve asked.

The man glared coolly up at him and ignored the question.

Without hesitation Steve planted a vicious blow in the man's face, splitting his nose and lip.

'Who sent you?' he repeated.

Moody licked his spouting lips but said nothing. Twice more Steve hit him then the gunman held up his hand in token of submission.

'We came to take you in for trial for killin' Ed Millard,' he said at length. 'Marshal Hart deputised us.'

Steve knew that was a lie but he didn't press things.

'Not getting much luck are you?' he grinned. 'Hart'll be needing some new deputies. The other two have just qualified for Boot Hill.'

There was disbelief in Moody's face for a

moment then the fact that he was sitting in the Pownall's living-room with the stranger in calm command registered. He swallowed hard a couple of times and eyed the glass in Steve's hand. Steve handed it over and Moody tossed the raw spirit down in a gulp. Both Mrs Pownall and Dave flashed looks of surprise at Steve but his words minimised the action.

'I guess you'll need that to give you the gall to account for your failure to the one who sent you,' he said slowly. 'Now get going. I'll give you a hand to drape your sidekicks on to their broncs.'

Moody stood up a little shakily and went to the door with Steve close behind him. Dave followed and fixed the door so that the light spread out into the compound. The gunman stared at the bodies of his cronies as though mesmerised and Steve had to jerk him into action. He took the dead men's guns away, handed them to Dave, then prodded Moody.

'Come on! Get this blamed carrion off the spread.'

Moody came out of his stupor and between them they draped the corpses over the saddle pommels.

'Where's your cayuse?' asked Steve.

Moody nodded towards the rising ground to the rear of the ranch-house. Steve laughed in a way that had Moody's nerves tingling.

'Reckon you're gonna ride double then. Take your choice. I guess neither will be much company for you.'

Moody fastened the lead rein of the horse carrying Brasher's body to the cantle of the other horse, and climbing into the saddle with the other body draped in front of him he rode off without a word.

When the sounds of hoofbeats faded Steve and Dave returned inside the ranch-house. Mrs Pownall had coffee boiling up and brought them both mugs of the steaming liquid. She took a chair opposite Steve and regarded him doubtfully.

'When that man hits town Mister Sherman, there'll be a small army hotfooting it after your blood,' she said. 'You'd better get on the move fast. I don't think they'll do us any harm so don't risk yourself by staying.'

Steve drained his mug and stood up. He evaded Dave's eyes as he answered.

'That's mighty good advice Ma'am. Guess I just got around to thinking the same thing.' He set his mug down, then going to the room where he'd hoped to sleep he hauled on his slicker and packed his warbag. A couple of minutes later he rejoined the Pownalls. He paused briefly then made towards the door. Dave watched him dumbly but Mrs Pownall smiled nervously.

'Good-bye Mister Sherman and thank you,' she said. Steve smiled in response, waved his free hand and went out to saddle his pinto. When he rode away he headed south on the trail to Blundell.

A thin moon edged up over the eastern skyline shedding a wan light over the undulating prairie. After an hour's easy riding he saw Moody and his grisly companions breasting a rise. He guided his pinto off the trail and made a wide detour, increasing the animal's pace so as to reach town ahead of the gunman.

Skirting Blundell he entered the town from the south. It was an hour after midnight but life was still going strong. Every saloon was lit and noisy. From two or three of them the discordant strains of pianos being played by drunken men merged with the general hubbub. Steve rode down the middle of Main Street and turned his mount into the shadows between the bank and Al Dunnett's store opposite Maxim's. He dismounted and stood beside the horse with one hand resting on the saddle pommel.

For about half an hour all he saw was a succession of half-drunk punchers staggering from one saloon to another and a few more clambering unsteadily into the saddles of their sleepy broncs and heading out of town. Then in rode Moody.

The slim wiry gunman slid out of the saddle and tied the lead rein to the hitch-rail before pushing his way into Maxim's. There was a brief interval when things went quiet in the big saloon then a stream of men came through the batwing doors to prove the veracity of Moody's statements.

Behind the crowd of punchers and townsfolk, framed in the light from the doorway, stood the two men who Steve had passed when leaving town en route for the Pownalls'. The one he now knew to be Marsh. The pair stood looking over the crowd, aloof and showing only slight interest. There were plenty of questions being bandied about but Steve failed to pick up any specific conversation until Marsh stepped forward to the sidewalk rail.

'They're not going to wake up no matter what noise you make,' he said. 'Get 'em to the funeral parlour. Neither of 'em was worth a crowd before they got killed.'

The crowd split up, leaving a clear passage, and Moody led the two horses bearing the dead men through and on up the street towards the funeral parlour. Most of the crowd followed but a few returned to Maxim's in the wake of Marsh and his companion.

After checking his guns Steve led the pinto across to the hitch-rail and after tethering the animal mounted the sidewalk and pushed open the batwing doors of Maxim's. He stood for a moment surveying the occupants. About twenty men sat around five tables playing cards. A few more sat singly, bottles and glasses in front of them. The pianist had given up playing and had both hands on a large pewter mug. Marshal Hart stood at one end of the bar with a tall showily-dressed young cowboy and the remaining few dance hostesses. In the centre of the bar Abe Marsh and his companion stared back at him.

Calmly Steve walked up to the bar. Marshal Hart turned and stared, his mouth dropping open in astonishment. He made a half-hearted attempt to reach for his gun then thought better of it and turned back to his drink. Steve stopped alongside Marsh and asked the barkeep for rye. He drank the first glass straight and pushed the empty back over the bar for a refill.

Marsh's cold eyes were roving over him but Steve ignored them and built himself a smoke. Long minutes went by with the tension building up inside Steve, but his features gave no sign. The barkeep refilled his glass and as he turned to take it he saw Marsh's companion nod briefly then he met Marsh's glance and grinned. There was no answering smile on Marsh's features.

'My name's Marsh. I didn't get your moniker.' The man's voice was deceptively casual. 'You forgot to say when you rubbed out Ed Millard and hightailed it outa town.'

'Sherman – Steve Sherman,' Steve answered easily. 'Can't see that I was under any obligation to spill my name around. In fact what's it to do with you?'

A glitter came into Marsh's eyes. The name seemed to hold some memory for him but he contained himself. Steve caught the look that Marsh's companion flashed him and his skin crawled. There was a quality in the man's expression that was totally evil and for all his lack of size Steve reckoned he'd have his way in any gathering. Marsh caught Steve's glance at his companion.

'I'm always interested in people, Sherman,' Marsh replied. 'Especially hombres who can use their six-guns like you.' He nodded towards his companion. 'This is Lew Fallon, my pardner.' Steve gave him a brief nod. 'Now under ordinary circumstances I'd be keen to get level with the man who rubbed out three of my hands in less than a day, but I guess they stepped outa line and I don't aim to be awkward.'

Steve looked unimpressed and took a sip at his drink before replying.

'Sure glad to hear your opinion Mister Marsh. I reckon your sayso will be enough to prise that two-bit Marshal out of wanting to tote me to the chokey.'

Marsh nodded coolly. 'You looking for work Sherman?' he asked.

Steve set his glass down and turned full on

to Marsh and Fallon.

'If you're aiming to offer me a steady forty and found job punching your beef you can save your breath,' he said, his lips curling in a sneer. 'I'll rub along on my own and find my own kinda work where I want it. Anyhow I don't think you'd be the sorta boss I could work for even if I did want something steady.'

'Howso?' Marsh drawled the question, his handsome face tense with anger.

'I like any boss o' mine to be particular who he hires. From what I've seen to date, it looks like you'll hire anyone who totes a gun.'

Marsh didn't rise to the bait. Instead he grinned easily.

'Guess I asked for your opinion Sherman so I can't beef now I've heard it.' The grin faded. 'But if you're not going to work for me I suggest you move on. No one else in Blundell will be taking on hands.'

'I said I'll rub along, remember?' put in Steve. 'And I don't aim to leave these parts until I'm good and ready.'

'Or dead!'

Those were the first words Steve had heard from Fallon and the man's hooded eyes gave the impression that the subject was the only one he savoured.

'That a challenge?' Steve drawled the words. His skin prickled as the man's lids rose slowly to show the eyes of a born killer; but the steadiness with which he regarded Fallon gave no evidence of his revulsion.

Fallon rested his glance briefly on Steve then away again to his glass.

'Nope, just a statement,' he said quietly. 'Just pointing out you've got two chances same as most folk.'

Steve set his glass on the bar counter and nodded to the barkeep to fill it, then with the full glass he moved a couple of yards away from Marsh and Fallon to indicate he'd done with talking. Marsh surveyed him thoughtfully but Fallon seemed to have inner problems claiming his attention.

The doors swung open and in walked Moody. His pock-marked face changed colour at the sight of Steve. The scars stood out livid and his mouth dropped open in astonishment. He shot a surprised look at Marshal Hart who still kept a discreet distance, then at Marsh for guidance. Steve eased gently away from the bar and waited for the next move.

It took a long time for Moody to reach a decision but at last the stiffness went out of his body and he came on up to the bar between Fallon and the group around Hart. He ordered a drink and turned his back on Steve who shrugged, drained his drink and started on out of the saloon.

At a table set halfway between the bar and

the batwing doors a rotund oldster with grey moustache and sidechops sat punishing a bottle of bourbon. He had a straw sticking out of the side of his mouth which he chewed between drinks. As Steve drew alongside his table he looked up. Steve felt keen brown eyes surveying him then the oldster motioned him to take a seat. He gave the old feller a grin and dragged a chair round to a position where he could keep the rest of Maxim's customers in view.

'Heard a bit of your conversation young feller,' the oldster said. 'My moniker's Tom Digby. I run a stage line from here to El Reno but unless I can get me a dyed-in-the-wool teamster mighty soon I guess the business'll be a dead duck.' He took a long drink and smacked his lips a time or two before continuing. 'My last three drivers got 'emselves killed by hold-up men and the guards that rode along went the same way. You interested?'

'Seems like the odds on living through to payday's pretty slim,' answered Steve. 'I like steadier work and a chance to spend the dinero I earn.'

Digby looked disappointed and his jowls drooped a little. 'I kinda hoped the way you talked to those jaspers an' the way you've handled the gunmen laying for you that you'd like a job where the chances of action seemed good.'

40

'Nope. I guess you've got me figured wrong Mister,' said Steve softly. 'It's the quiet life I like and I never push for trouble. Howcome you're still in business after these hold-ups? Folk must be mighty patient to send freight with you still.'

'The hold-up gang were plumb unlucky every time,' grinned Digby. 'There was no freight aboard each time they horned in. A coupla passengers got 'emselves parted from some dinero but not so much that it hurts, an' one feller who turned out to be a lawman got himself salivated going for his shooting iron.'

Steve nodded slowly. 'Anybody see the lawman go for his guns? A good lawman mostly backs down when the cards are stacked against him.'

'Yeah. Kurt Munro, the rodeo rider. That's the flashy dresser talking to Hart an' Moody.'

Steve let his eyes rest on Munro for a moment then looked back at Digby. He rolled a cigarette while he considered things.

'Reckon I'd like to think it over a piece Digby before telling you one way or another. What bothers me is that driving a stage is one sure way of letting folk know just where you're gonna be at any given time an' the way I've made enemies hereabouts makes it plumb foolish to advertise my location.'

Digby's jowls lifted and a smile edged his

41

lips as he replied.

'You'll have no cause to worry Sherman. Once I can let it be known you'll take the stage there'll be plenty o' good men who'll be glad to ride guard. I guess the raiders'll think twice before trying another hold-up, an' Marsh's men'll fight shy of laying for you.'

Steve didn't answer and Tom Digby's shrewd eyes regarded him closely.

'Well, you think it over Sherman. The pay's sixty a month an' your keep thrown in if you stay at my place. If you ain't fixed up a room you're welcome to stay with me an' my gal while you make up your mind.'

'I'll take you up on that Digby,' replied Steve. 'I reckon Marsh runs the hotel and I'd have to sleep with both eyes open there.'

A big smile settled on Digby's face, and corking the bottle in front of him, he slipped it into his pocket and stood up.

'C'mon,' he said. 'You can stable your cayuse at my place.'

Steve nodded and followed the oldster out. He kept Marsh and his underlings under surveillance until he pushed his way through the doors, but they seemed to have forgotten his existence and took no apparent notice of his departure. As he followed Digby to the staging depot he tried again to puzzle out just where he had seen Marsh before but his memory failed him. He gave it up at length content in the knowledge that something would jolt his mind back to the occasion.

CHAPTER THREE

Steve pulled his chair back and reached for the makings. The breakfast he had just eaten had been cooked to the finest degree of perfection and he had eaten to the limit of his capacity.

During weeks of lone travelling, living out of cans or on what he could forage and hard tack, he was quite content and had no thought of lush living; but when opportunity presented itself, he enjoyed a good, well-cooked meal.

Claire Digby came out of the kitchen at the sound of Steve's chair scraping back. She cast a quizzical eye at him and Steve smiled back.

'That was mighty fine Ma'am,' he said. 'You're sure some cook.'

A brief smile of pleasure lit her face, momentarily transforming austere features into radiant good looks. The difference was so remarkable that a moment later Steve wondered whether the transformation was no more than a trick of his imagination. As she came forward with the coffee pot in her hands to pour out cups for both of them, he studied her features carefully.

Her skin was browned by the Texas sun and her jet black hair was pulled back tightly and held in one long pigtail. Big brown eyes looked out from under neat black eyebrows, her nose was straight and small and her mouth had perfect shape. Indeed she had all the ingredients of beauty. She was dressed in a dark green blouse and brown riding skirt and these severe garments both failed to disguise the excellence of her figure.

Steve looked away guiltily as the slow flush that started at her neck told him that she had been aware of his scrutiny. He stammered a bit before making conversation.

'Y – Your pa sure got away to an early start Ma'am,' he said at length. 'Anything to do with the running of the stage?'

Claire sat down opposite him and took a sip of the scalding coffee before replying.

'He's gone down to El Reno to ask for more time to get the stage running again.'

She cast a quick worried look up at him but for all her concern about her father's business she could not help her thoughts digressing as her glance took in Steve's handsome face and the set of his muscular shoulders. The flush started creeping up her neck again as she continued.

'If we don't run into El Reno in four days'

time the contract will be scrapped then it will be thrown open to anyone who wants to take over, that's unless Wells Fargo decide to operate themselves. I've heard that Marsh is all set to take the line over.'

'It looks just a heap o' trouble to me,' Steve remarked. 'Can't see any business being worth the number of men who've died running it recently.'

Claire flushed hotly as the implication of Steve's remark stung her and Steve decided he liked her angry.

'My father doesn't take men's lives lightly Mister Sherman.' Her voice was edged with ice and Steve kept his smile back with difficulty. 'But he's run this business a long time and up to now it's paid well. We carry a lot of traffic between El Reno and Fort Dexter at Mochita.'

'Mochita, eh?' mused Steve. 'That's across the Red River on the south-west corner of the Nation. Haven't the military from Fort Dexter done anything about the hold-ups and range trouble hereabouts?'

'No, I guess that new Marshal reckons he can handle things. Anyway, the Indians keep the military at full stretch. They're always threatening to burst out of the Nation and now and again Black Eagle's braves get out on the loose.' The girl paused and flashed a quick glance at Steve. 'Are you seriously thinking of taking over the run?'

'I always think seriously about any proposition I get,' replied Steve pushing his mug over for a refill. Claire drained hers and refilled both. 'But this is the first offer I've had to take over a stage-run and it would need careful thought even if the survival chances were better. Anyway, I'm not so sure I want to take sides in Blundell. I do better for myself ploughing a lone furrow.'

'How do you mean?' Claire asked then looked away in embarrassment as she realised she was prying into his affairs. Steve smiled away her discomfiture.

'When you spend your life riding into the skyline, you hit a lot of towns and every one of 'em spells trouble if you take sides. It's the same everywhere – someone growing out of his graze, pushing the small fry for all he's worth and running the town. I reckon a man could get himself salivated in any one of a hundred towns just by taking sides.'

'I guess that's your way of telling me we're taking our troubles too personally,' Claire replied. 'Maybe you're right Mister Sherman. It could be a thousand other people are faced with the same problems but one thing's for sure, they're all as concerned as I am; but you're right not to take sides. The trouble was here before you hit town. You're under no obligation one way or another.' She waited a moment while he lit his cigarette, and eyeing his calm detached manner she felt a sudden surge of anger. 'Maybe after consideration you've decided the prospects are better working for Marsh?'

Steve made no attempt to deny the accusation contained in her remark but instead drew deeply on his cigarette. His expression gave no indication of his thoughts and Claire stood up abruptly, commencing to gather the dishes together. He watched the rapid rise and fall of her breasts as she struggled with her anger until his conscience made him drop his eyes.

'This lawman that died on one of the hold-ups,' he said as Claire came out of the kitchen for the remainder of the dishes. 'I guess you or your pa recovered his possessions. Who was he?'

A new thought crossed the girl's mind. Perhaps Sherman was on the run. Her eyes narrowed as she considered her reply but she decided the truth would have to do.

'The hold-up men took everything he owned except a United States Deputy Marshal's badge.'

'Did you get to know what he looked like?' Steve persisted.

'I saw his body when the stage pulled in the depot,' Claire answered. 'He looked sort of medium build, red hair, small featured with a scar across his forehead.'

There was a solemn faraway look on Steve's face and Claire concluded that he knew the lawman only too well. She had the immediate feeling that the lawman's business had been Steve Sherman and the wall of reserve started building up in her.

'That Munro. I heard tell he was there when the lawman got his. How come Munro's alive to tell the tale?'

Steve judged by the hot red flush flooding the girl's face, she had done some thinking about Munro. He was a good-looker, that was for sure and Steve reckoned he must have stood out a bit from the general run of roughnecks like the real thing from fools' gold.

'I guess Kurt saw it was useless to buck the odds. One more dead man wouldn't have helped. He brought the stage in after.'

Steve nodded stiffly. For some unaccountable reason the ease with which she had used Munro's first name set his temper alight. He stood up abruptly and turned to face the girl.

'Looks like he's the man to take the stage over. He's got the knack of staying alive while other men die.' He paused and returned the girl's hard stare. 'I'm mighty obliged to you Ma'am for an excellent breakfast but I guess I'll be riding on.'

Claire nodded woodenly but refrained from saying anything while Steve collected his warbag and made his way out to the stables at the rear. Shortly after, on the trail to El Reno, he grinned and scratched his head in perplexity at his reactions to a girl's natural interest in a young good-looking rodeo rider.

It was nearly nightfall when he guided his tired pinto into the long main street of El Reno. The Wells Fargo office was well lighted and as he rode past he saw three men talking, one of them Tom Digby. It looked like Digby was finding the going hard to arrange an extension. He rode on until he came abreast of the Sheriff's shingle. Tethering his horse to the hitch-rail he mounted the sidewalk and pushed the gaol-house door open. A whipcord tough oldster with large dangling grey moustaches and keen blue eyes looked up from his desk and surveyed his visitor coolly. He nodded to a chair at the end of the table and waited for Steve to start talking.

Digging into his shirt pocket Steve placed a gleaming silver badge in front of the oldster. The Sheriff looked closely at it then back at Steve who returned the badge to his shirt pocket.

'The name's Sherman, Steve Sherman,' Steve said, nodding when the Sheriff pointed to the bottle of bourbon that took pride of place on the table. 'Before leaving Dallas I checked on you, and I take it you're John Dean.'

'That's right.' Dean's voice was a bit thick

49

as he answered and Steve reckoned he'd been pretty busy with the bottle for a long time. There was nothing wrong with the steadiness of the Sheriff's hand though as he poured out two measures. 'You got anything special on your mind?'

Steve reached out for his glass and nodded.

'Yeah. All that sudden death and violence that's broken out over your territory.'

Dean's eyes were guarded as he looked at Steve.

'I don't remember hollerin' for help,' he growled. 'I've been Sheriff of Reno County for the last ten years an' never once asked for help.'

'Maybe you haven't done much riding lately,' put in Steve quietly. 'Mog Myers, the marshal of Blundell, stopped a bullet before he could holler. Things have been mighty rough in Blundell. Plenty of dead men, and good men put out of business. Digby's Stage got shot up three times in the last few months.'

'Yeah, I know,' snarled Dean. He tossed his drink back and glared across at Steve. 'But nobody's beefed to me an' another Marshal got voted in. He reckons he's got his fingers on the trouble.'

'Who pays you to take his word for it?' Steve snapped the question and for a brief moment fire kindled in Dean's eyes. The fire went out and the Sheriff's shoulders sagged.

'Nobody pays me Mister Sherman,' he said at length. 'But I reckon I'm plumb fed up with ridin'. I've ridden on trouble shootin' routine for nigh on thirty years an' now the sight of a cayuse brings up goose pimples on my callouses.'

'That's what I figured,' Steve answered. 'A feller gets tired. You've got a good record Dean up to the time you stopped riding. But a mighty tough crowd have muscled in on your territory, ready and eager to take advantage of a chair-bound Sheriff.'

Dean tossed another drink down his throat to help digest the unpleasant truth contained in the young United States Marshal's statement. He lit up a cheroot in a harassed sort of manner.

'Y'know Sheriff,' Steve went on. 'It's no crime to get too old to enjoy riding the lone trails. I guess we all get that way too soon but when things get too hot to handle it's the duty of any Sheriff to get help.'

'It's like I said. Nobody's complained,' Dean grated.

'Somebody did,' said Steve, his bright eyes fixing on Dean's face. 'A letter came to the office at Dallas and a Deputy by the name of Ellis came to check on things. He was gunned down on the Blundell Stage. We had no word from Ellis so I've been sent to find out what's happened.'

There was a blank expression on the Sheriff's face and he pulled hard on his cheroot.

'There was no lawman on the stage to my knowledge. How come you're so sure?'

'Digby's daughter told me. They dug his badge out of a pocket the stage robbers had missed.'

'Then why in heck didn't Digby tell me?' Dean exploded.

Before Steve could reply the door opened and a slim girl in her early twenties with flaming red hair came in with a tray covered over by a clean cloth. She looked at Steve hesitantly then smiled returning his nod. He noticed her eyes were grey, flecked with brown and her lips wide and generous. He stood up as she placed the tray on the table. He caught the look of affection that sprang into Sheriff Dean's eyes as he thanked the girl and at once knew why the Sheriff had given up riding.

'This is Steven Sherman,' Dean said eyeing the plate which contained a succulent looking grill. 'My gal, Myra.'

'I'm sure pleased to make your acquaintance Miss Myra,' Steve murmured and Myra Dean smiled back at him with a complete lack of affectation. She held out her hand, losing it in Steve's big palm. In the brief space of time it took to shake hands he noticed how cool and possessed she was, as though she had an inner spark that satisfied all her wants.

'He's a U.S. Marshal Myra,' continued the Sheriff. 'I guess he's come to do the chore I should've had done long ago.'

'You've done plenty in your time father,' Myra said quickly. Her voice had a depth and quality that Steve found fascinating. She turned to Steve and fixed him with a look that promised plenty of fireworks if her opinion wasn't acceptable. 'My father made El Reno safe for law abiding citizens a long time ago and that goes for all the territory in the county including Blundell. He cleared out killers, rustlers and Indians. Now years later the killers and rustlers have come back but the citizens are too easy to make a stand against them. It seems there's a profit in lawlessness that they want to share in. Years ago my father could get a posse together at the drop of a hat but now they're too busy selling bad hooch and stores to killers. Well, my father's not riding alone. The odds are too great.'

Dean cast a quick look at Steve but said nothing. He was obviously waiting for Steve's reaction before saying his piece. Steve nodded and his face softened as he glanced at the girl who so quickly defended her father. He concluded there couldn't be much wrong with a man who engendered this sort of affection.

'Yeah. I guess it all adds up to what you

say Miss Myra. But maybe between us we'll clear up the territory again.'

'I'll give you any help I can young feller,' said Dean after spearing a piece of kidney from his plate. 'But there's mighty powerful bosses at the back of things hereabouts an' I'm thinking we'll need a durned sight more than two of us to get things cleaned up.'

Myra was looking guiltily at the meal her father was starting in to eat.

'Would you like me to rustle up something for you to eat Mister Sherman?' she asked.

Steve shook his head. 'No thank you. No need to go to any trouble. I'll have something in the local chop house as soon as I stable my cayuse. I'll be moving on at sunup but I'd sure appreciate using one of your cells for the night.'

'We've got room,' put in the girl. 'You can stay at the house and stable your horse at the back of the gaol.'

'Nope, I'll sleep in a cell,' Steve answered. 'But I'm obliged to you for your consideration.'

He went outside without waiting for further argument and returned a minute later with his warbag. Myra unhooked some keys from a nail in the wall and led the way through to the cells. She unlocked the nearest and Steve went in, placing his bag on the floor. He tested the bunk with his hand and grinned at the girl.

'Many's the night when this would have seemed like heaven,' he said.

'I guess so,' Myra replied drily.

'I'll see to my cayuse now then catch up with some shut-eye. I guess your father and me can palaver in the morning.'

He spent a long time looking after his pinto and ate a meal at a nearby kitchen. Coming back he exchanged a few words with Dean before turning in. Myra Dean had not been content to let him sleep like a prisoner but had made up his bunk with sheets and pillowcases. As he lay between the sheets later smoking a last cigarette, he found himself comparing the red-haired Myra with Claire Digby. For a man who had previously given little thought to women he decided it was a strange pastime and hardly in keeping with the assignment before him, but he fell off to sleep still thinking of them.

He awoke at the first flush of dawn to the sound of the gaol-house door opening. Stifling a yawn he sat up in his bunk as a woman's footsteps padded through the office and into the cell block. Myra Dean pushed the cell door open and placed a tray covered with a cloth on the white scrubbed table. Steve's nose wrinkled appreciatively as the tang of freshly brewed coffee seeped from under the cloth. He grinned in pleasure at Myra who, although dressed in a lilac print dress of simple cut, looked the picture of healthy feminine beauty.

'That's mighty good of you ma'am,' Steve said. 'I guess being a prisoner in this hoosegow would have its compensations.'

Myra laughed. 'Prisoners don't get my personal attention so don't take to crime under a misapprehension.' She took the cloth from the tray, poured a mug of coffee out of the jug and handed it to him. 'I thought maybe you'd be riding early and men never seem to get around to eating properly unless the cooking's done for them.'

'Yeah. I guess you're right but that doesn't mean you've gotta worry on my account,' Steve replied after taking a sip of the scalding liquid. The good humour faded a little from Myra's eyes and he was quick to continue. 'I'm mighty glad you did though. That breakfast sure looks good enough to eat.'

'I'll leave you to it then,' she said, her humour restored. She turned at the cell door as Steve called to her.

'Just in case I don't see you or the Sheriff again before I hit the trail I'll be glad if you'll keep my job dark. I guess the less folks know hereabouts, the better.'

'We'll say nothing Mister Sherman,' Myra promised. Her glance lingered a moment on his handsome features and wide shoulders, then she was gone and Steve slid out of the bunk to start in on the mixed grill and wheat cakes.

Half an hour later he led his pinto out of the stable at the rear of the gaol-house and springing into the saddle headed out of town on the north trail for Blundell. El Reno, bathed in the red glow of the early morning sun, still slept. The only visible sign that the day's business had commenced was the Fargo Stage drawn up outside the office and facing south. A couple of sleepy-eyed passengers stared out stupidly as Steve swept past.

He rode at a steady pace, keeping his eager mount in check. The animal was beautifully proportioned and seemingly tireless but Steve always reckoned to keep plenty of fire in reserve. He never knew when his life might depend upon a burst of the electrifying speed that the pinto could muster.

The trail was clogged with dust and the grassland siding it looked parched and tired. Already the sun shone with pitiless intensity, burning its way through his thick woollen shirt, and the sweat ran in tiny rivulets down his face.

Hardened to these minor discomforts Steve took stock of the terrain. Away to east and west the land rolled in undulating fashion like a calcified sea until the shimmering heat haze formed a skyline, but to the north big hills lorded over a huddle of foothills hiding the many tributaries of the Red River that irrigated the verdant grasslands around Blundell.

He remembered that the trail ran for a couple of miles along a narrow valley between two humped hills and guessed that this point had been used by the hold-up men. The hills were serried by gaps and narrow canyons affording shelter and easy escape for a small army of bandits. No wonder Digby was finding it hard to rustle up a crew for his stage-coach.

These thoughts brought the youngster Ellis back into his mind. The Deputy Marshal had been a cheerful likeable lawman with a promising future; and now he was dead. It didn't do to dwell on such things but Steve only managed to push the thought aside to have the memory of his elder brother Sam Sherman take its place.

Sam's death had been a mighty big blow to Steve. Sam, ten years older than Steve, had been a U.S. Marshal a few years when he was found beside a burned-out stage-coach, riddled with bullets. The driver and guard had been picked up not far away both fatally wounded. The guard managed to tell how the other passenger, dressed in clergyman's garb, must have pulled a gun on Sam who was taking the Laredo Kid to Fort Concho.

Armed with the Marshal's guns the Laredo Kid climbed atop the stage and forced the driver to stop. Disarmed they watched while Sam Sherman was ordered outside. The Kid emptied the magazine of one gun into the helpless lawman then instructed the driver and guard to get walking. Just when it seemed they were getting out unscathed, a hail of bullets scythed them down. The pseudo clergyman and the Laredo Kid then set fire to the stage and rode off with the team.

Just a couple of days before Sam met his death he had stopped with his prisoner for a few hours at the Shermans' ranch, the Box S, and Steve well remembered the occasion when the lawman had prodded the Laredo Kid into the stage that was to take them on the first leg of the journey to Fort Concho. The Kid's face had been covered with a thick overgrowth of beard and moustaches, making expression difficult to read, but the eyes that had lingered on Sam as he climbed into the coach spelled hate and murder.

It had been Steve's intention to follow in his brother's footsteps and hunt the Laredo Kid until vengeance was his but a report had drifted in just after he had become a Deputy Marshal that Colston Clay, the Sheriff of Tascosa, had cornered Laredo in a line shack after the Tascosa bank had been robbed. The Kid had finally set the shack on fire an hour or so before dawn and when the fire subsided the Sheriff had found the charred remains of three men, one of whom, matching the size of Laredo, had items of clothing still recognisable in part as having belonged to the Kid.

The proceeds of the bank robbery had never been recovered so it looked like the Kid had had the last laugh, albeit a bitter one.

For a long time Steve had cursed Colston Clay for having robbed him of his revenge but he mellowed, becoming content in the knowledge that the law had eventually prevailed.

He pictured again the Laredo Kid and his memory played tricks as the figure of Abe Marsh became superimposed on it. The images stayed with him and he drew his pinto to a stop to roll himself a smoke as he considered the similarity of the two men. The build, allowing for a little thickening, was the same, and the eyes and eyebrows could have belonged to the same man. Steve drew deeply on his cigarette and a slow smile edged his lips as he decided it was within his powers to prove one way or another whether in fact Marsh was the Laredo Kid. He sat quietly in the saddle a long time, hardly noticing the increasing heat of the sun, allowing the hate of years to seep through him. At length, when he urged his pinto forward, his face was grim and purpose showed in every line of his supple body.

CHAPTER FOUR

When Steve turned his mount down into the narrow valley between the long-humped foothills, a rider below drew his horse swiftly off the trail and into one of the countless crevices that scarred the hills throughout their length. In the brief space of time horse and rider were in view Steve recognised them. He had admired Val Trent's big albino mare many times before and he and Trent, the Wells Fargo trouble shooter, were old friends. He grinned as he pictured Val, flattened against the rock face, his Colt already held firmly in his deadly left hand. Trent never took chances and had built himself a reputation for wide-awake attention to business at all times.

Steve kept the pinto moving steadily down the grade and when he was almost level with the split rock face Val's voice spat out the harsh command.

'Keep coming Mister and keep away from the hardware!' There was a pause then the delighted shout: 'Steve you old side-winder! What in tarnation are you doing here?'

'Hiya Val!' returned Steve, a smile of pleasure on his face as Trent moved out of hiding. Sliding out of the saddle he shook hands with the husky blond Fargo man then felt in his shirt pocket for the makings.

'We got word of troubles around this territory,' said Steve at length when they sat and smoked in the shade of an overhanging rock. 'And Ellis one of our men, was sent to check on things. We got no word from Ellis and that's how it was when I got back from a chore in El Paso, so I got orders to find out what happened to Ellis.'

Trent's ruggedly handsome face was serious as he listened. His deep blue eyes searched Steve's face for a moment and seeing the lawman's set expression he nodded his understanding.

'Looks like you found out what happened to Ellis?'

'Yeah, he got shot down in one of those stage hold-ups. I reckon they knew him for what he was. You been around here long Val?'

'Nope. Just drifted into El Reno yesterday. Got sent up from Austin to spy out the trail to the Nation and to make sure the stage carrying the half-yearly pay-off for the Indians gets through without any trouble.'

Steve pondered this for some time. 'Some chore,' he said at length.

Trent shrugged. 'Never found a chore yet that was better than the last one. Wells Fargo are responsible for seeing the dinero reaches its destination. In the past the responsibility could be passed on to Digby at El Reno but not any more. Whether a Digby or a Fargo stage leaves El Reno with the dinero aboard, I've gotta see it arrives.'

'Looks like we can work together then,' said Steve. 'It's my guess that your stage jumpers are the same hombres who've been causing all the hell around Blundell. Boss man of the outfit calls himself Abe Marsh. He's sided by a natural killer type, name of Lew Fallon, and a whole bunch of gunmen. Marsh drove a trail herd into the Blundell free graze some time ago and stayed on. He's pushed all the small ranchers so hard that there's no one left to fight. His crew rule the roost and now Marsh has got Blundell in a strangle hold.'

'You got anything on Marsh?' queried Trent.

It was a long time before Steve shook his head and Val guessed that the negation held some reserve.

'One thing I know,' added Steve. 'Marsh is gonna be a mighty hard man to beat. He's got plenty of control and nobody's gonna push him into going for the hardware unless he holds the aces. He runs a trigger-happy crew all too keen to do his killing for him.'

The big blond man just grinned. It was a pattern he'd come to know only too well.

'I guess I'm not too popular with Marsh,'

63

continued Steve. 'A couple of his crew got itchy fingers and now he's short of some hands.'

'Howso?' asked Trent.

Steve lit a new cigarette from the stub of the old one and told Trent what had happened from the time of his arrival at Blundell. Trent gave him his full attention and smoked steadily until Steve finished his story.

'I reckon we're gonna have our hands full sorting things out on this range.' The Fargo man scratched his head but his expression held no vestige of perplexity.

'Yeah, and that's maybe some understatement,' grinned Steve. 'I'd kinda like to make things boil up plenty fast by taking a leaf out of Marsh's book and pushing a herd right on to the range he's hogging.' Steve paused then shook his head. 'I guess it'd take too long to get Lacey, the Box S foreman, to run a coupla hundred head up here with the boys.'

'Now that's a real bright notion Steve,' nodded Trent. 'As you say we haven't got the time for your boys to take a hand, but I passed a trail herd on the way into El Reno, bossed by a feller with plenty cause to back your play.'

Steve looked up sharply as Trent continued: 'Remember Jim Hammond, the youngster Matt James took off to bargain himself outa that shooting fracas on the Neuces?' Steve nodded. 'Well his pa, Li Hammond, ain't no more than twenty miles south-east o' here right now. I guess he'd be mighty tickled to help pay back some of the score.'

'Where's he heading?' asked Steve.

'Mochita. He's got the beef contract with the Indian Agent at Fort Dexter. This is the third run he's made and I guess a few days one way or the other ain't gonna make any difference to him. It ain't as though it's his first time.'

'Y'know Val, I think you've struck the answer to some of the problems. Li Hammond's a pretty tough hombre and runs a hard crew. I reckon they'd keep Marsh's men plenty busy.' Steve passed a hand over his face, rubbing away the sweat that still oozed out of his scalp as he stood up. 'I guess I'll mosey along right now and see what Hammond thinks of the idea.'

'There's no point in me riding along with you Steve,' Val Trent said, standing up. 'I'll cover the trail on into Blundell. Is there anything you'd like me to check on until you show up?'

'Yeah,' Steve said slowly. 'Mebbe the Pownalls haven't left the Lazy Y yet. You could tell 'em it's likely a trail herd will be grazing on their range in a coupla days with a crew of drovers all set to take up the battle with Marsh.'

Val Trent nodded and swung himself astride his albino horse. The pals waved a brief farewell and Steve set his horse up the grade back towards El Reno. Trent watched him go until the trail curved then he rode easily on his way to Blundell.

It was late afternoon when Steve saw the dust cloud in the distance that told him a trail herd was on the move. He reined in his sweating horse and slid out of the saddle to await the slow-moving herd. From his water canteen he measured out a drink for his horse, pouring it into his Stetson. The pinto drank delicately and then Steve drank sparingly, allowing a couple of mouthfuls to trickle slowly down his throat.

A speck that had been moving way out in front of the dust cloud materialised as a chuck wagon that rolled on beyond Steve, passing him at a distance of a couple of hundred yards. He felt himself under the close scrutiny of the driver, a spare man carrying a lot of black beard, but the man made no sign that he had observed Steve and the wagon was soon lost to sight behind a steep-sided hill.

The herd emerged out of the dust cloud, a compact, well disciplined herd, all following a big serene-looking steer that picked its pace like a real trail veteran. The drovers at point, although covered in alkali and sweating under the broiling heat of the sun, rode easily, seemingly quite content to leave things to the lead steer.

The left hand swing men passed Steve quite close and each man scrutinised him searchingly but none returned his greeting. He didn't recognise any of them but if Li Hammond was their boss, he reckoned they were all right. Then coming up with one of the flank riders was the man he'd come to meet.

Li Hammond, slim built but tough as a timber wolf, was riding an ugly coal-black mustang that looked to be made of muscle. He broke away from his companion to look closer at Steve then he set the mustang to close the distance at a gallop. The horse slithered to a stop and Hammond was out of the saddle in a trice. He advanced on Steve, a big smile cracking the dust that lay thick on his weather-beaten face.

'Steve Sherman!' he exclaimed, grasping Steve's palm in a grip like iron. 'My, this is sure enough a pleasant surprise.'

'Hiya Li!' grinned Steve. 'Val Trent told me you were in the territory so I reckoned to look you up.'

'Uh-uh,' Hammond grunted. 'I saw Val yesterday but he didn't say you were around.'

'Nope. We only met up today.'

'Say Steve, we'll be striking night camp

67

pretty soon now. How about riding along then we can palaver some?'

'Sure thing, that's what I came for,' Steve replied.

Hammond cast a shrewd glance at the lawman then with a grin he climbed aboard his mustang and waited for Steve to swing into his saddle before riding off towards the head of the herd. They caught up with the chuck wagon and rode alongside for a half-an-hour or so then when the driver hauled his team to a stop beside a clear slow-running stream, Steve and Hammond dismounted and supervised the intake of their thirsty horses. The stream swung around to the south-east in a wide arc and the herd was already spread along its length.

'It's not often that you find as handy a place to pitch camp,' remarked Hammond, watching his drovers bunching the herd after the animals had drunk their fill.

Steve nodded his agreement. 'I guess you're over the worst now Li,' he said. 'You shouldn't have much water shortage between here and Mochita.'

'Yeah, that's what I figured,' the trail boss replied.

They stood together, watching the cook busy himself with his hastily constructed field kitchen and the horse wrangler bringing in a couple of spirited cow ponies. There was an expression of deep satisfaction on

Hammond's face.

'Young Jim's growing up into a husky feller Steve,' he remarked, lighting up a cheroot. 'He was asking about you.'

'That lad's sure enough spunky Li. I reckon you'll be mighty proud of him. Say hello to him for me when you get back.'

Hammond nodded. He knew Steve had something to ask of him and by bringing alive his obligation tried to make it plain that Steve only had to ask. He drew deeply on his cheroot and turned to face Steve.

'I guess chow'll be ready pretty soon. Mebbe you can tell me what's on your mind while we're digesting old Dimond's poison.'

A few minutes later they sat with their backs against the steep side of the foothill eating a meal that was far from the poison Hammond had prophesied.

'I don't know how tight your schedule is Li,' Steve said at length. 'But there's a situation around Blundell that a trail herd manned by a tough crew could bring to the boil. It'd mebbe take a week.' He paused. 'It could be that some good men would die too.'

Hammond kept on eating for a long time. He nodded towards the drovers who rode in one after another to grab a meal.

'This is the toughest crew I've bossed Steve, and it's my guess they'd like it fine to have a chance of flexing their muscles before pushing on to Mochita. Suppose you tell me all about it.'

Steve grinned and lit up a cigarette before settling himself back comfortably. He gave Hammond the full story then waited for the trail boss's comments.

'Just where would you like me to push my herd?' Hammond asked.

'The Lazy Y,' replied Steve. 'I guess we could take over the ranch buildings as headquarters. I reckon we'd soon get the attention of Marsh and his crew.'

Hammond stood up and jerked his head to indicate that Steve should follow him. He walked on ahead of Steve to where a dozen drovers sat around the chuck wagon eating their well-earned meal. They all eyed Steve with curiosity but no one spoke. They seemed content to leave the talking to Hammond. Steve ran his eye over them swiftly and saw that Hammond had hand-picked his men. He didn't see a misfit amongst them.

'I'd like you fellers to meet an old pard o' mine, U.S. Deputy Marshal Steve Sherman.'

Most of the drovers nodded and a couple said 'Hiya'. Hammond sat down amongst them and motioned Steve to take a seat.

'Steve Sherman did me a mighty good turn a coupla years back and there isn't much I wouldn't do for him if he asked. He's come up against a pretty tough crew of killers in Blundell who brought a trail herd on to the free range and stayed on to rule the roost.

70

He'd like us to move in with the herd for a few days.' He paused but the drovers just carried on eating, waiting for him to continue. 'Well you fellers are all on a percentage of this herd and that gives you all a say. If we push the herd on the Blundell range we're mebbe gonna lose some steers and some of us could stay in Boot Hill.'

The prospect caused no alarm to show on the dust-lined faces in the circle. In fact the gleam of interest lit many pairs of eyes. They all looked towards a husky, black visaged man who sat opposite Hammond. One after another they nodded and a grin of satisfaction spread over his face.

'If you reckon Sherman's worth helping Li, then that's all right by us,' he said. 'I'll ride around the others and get their sayso.'

He stood up and pushed his plate into the pan of boiling water. As he walked towards his horse Hammond touched his shoulder and stopped him.

'I'd like you to meet our scout, Mike Ringold,' Hammond said, turning to Steve.

Steve stood up and shook hands with the man. He looked into a pair of fearless eyes that held a glint of humour.

'Mighty pleased to know you Mike,' he said. 'You sure carved a reputation for yourself as a lawman back in Arizona.'

Ringold shrugged and grinned. 'Ah, you know how it is Sherman. The lawman's

71

always got the edge in a fracas. Be seeing you.'

Steve turned to Hammond with a smile as Ringold went on his way. No wonder he had been content to leave the decision to his crew. With a fire-eater like Ringold amongst them he knew well enough they'd back him to the hilt.

About an hour later Ringold rode back in. He unsaddled his bronc unhurriedly and watered it before rejoining the men around the fire.

'They're all with you Li,' he said after biting off a sizeable chew of tobacco from a thick plug. 'Seems this herd's been so docile the fellers are ready for anything to change the monotony.'

A couple of the drovers guffawed. 'Docile he says!' a deep-chested man grated. 'Most ornery bunch of steers I ever did see. Only the last coupla days they decided at last to keep headin' north. It's a rest from the blamed critturs I'm lookin' forward to.'

Steve stayed on chatting for a couple of hours getting to know each member of Hammond's outfit. Before leaving he drew a map in the dust, showing the route to the Lazy Y. Ringold studied it for a while then smoothed the dust over.

'We'll be grazin' on Lazy Y pasture afore nightfall tomorrow,' he said coolly.

'Suits me,' replied Steve getting to his feet.

'Well, I'll be moseying on. Be seeing you.'

The rest of the crew waved a farewell and Hammond crossed to where Steve's pinto grazed.

'I sure hope things turn out the way you want them Steve,' he said when at length Steve was in the saddle.

'Yeah, I'm a mite more optimistic now that you're taking sides.' They shook hands and Steve rode off in to the gathering gloom.

The moon was up when he hit the Blundell trail, it's dim light bringing into silhouette the rider his horse had already warned him was in the vicinity. Straining his eyes he came to the conclusion that the rider ahead was either a woman or a lightly built man, and travelling fast. Steve, his curiosity mounting, raised his pinto's gait.

The trail curved taking the rider out of view and as Steve rounded the bend he palmed one of his guns. The horse in front had stopped. The moon was strong enough for him to recognise immediately the girl who sat her mount plumb in the middle of the trail holding a gun pointed unerringly at his midriff. It was the Sheriff's daughter, Myra Dean.

'Stay right there, Mister!' Her voice was agitated but not frightened, then as her knowledge of his identity dawned upon her: 'Oh, it's you Mister Sherman. I guess I can put the gun away.'

Steve holstered his own gun and rode in close.

'What the heck are you doing riding this trail at night-time Miss Myra?'

'You can well ask.' There was bitterness in the girl's voice. 'Your talk of duty so unsettled my father that not long after you left he saddled up and went riding into Blundell. I got tired of biting my nails so I decided to get where I could keep an eye on him.'

'And so you're riding into Blundell?' Steve's reply was sharp. 'And what good's a lawman gonna do who's got a woman on his tail? If you give a man enough to worry over he'd lose a gun battle no matter how good he is.'

He saw her head fly up and pictured the grey eyes flashing.

'You can't transfer the blame to me Mister Sherman,' she ground out. 'You're the one who prodded him into taking chances he's no longer fit to take. Oh why couldn't you have stayed away just a few months more then he'd have been finished with it all.'

Steve wasn't prepared to argue or excuse himself for doing his duty.

'No use palavering here Ma'am,' he said stiffly. 'If you're going to Blundell then I guess we'd better ride together. That's where I'm heading anyway.'

Without waiting for a reply he gigged his mount into action. He didn't look back but

74

heard the hoofbeats of Myra's horse as she followed him. For several miles they rode in single file then at last the desire for company was too strong and she rode alongside him. Steve glanced now and again at the girl but she remained stiff-lipped and kept her eyes straight ahead on the trail. The moon had gathered strength, its kindly light giving her face an ethereal quality and softening the contours of her lissom figure. He felt his pulse rate quicken as her beauty impressed itself upon him and he had to be firm with himself to stop sneaking glances. After a few miles when he eventually looked at her again, she was looking his way. There was a half-smile on her face and their mutual tension went.

For the rest of the way into Blundell they talked on general topics and Steve found himself comparing the girl with Claire Digby. Myra Dean was the complete product of the Texan range, beautiful but wiry, direct of speech and without guile, a woman who would stand four-square behind her man and if need be, in front of him. Claire Digby, probably more beautiful, had an air of intangible mystery, a depth that excited and stirred the imagination, a way of comporting herself that had the unmistakable tag of eastern seaboard schooling. He didn't get anywhere with the comparison and reckoned he was a darned lucky guy that he'd be moving on when his chore was done. The girls would no doubt cause some other feller plenty of heart-searching before he plumped for the wrong one.

'You've been mighty quiet for a while Mister Sherman. What's on your mind?' Myra's voice jerked Steve out of his reverie.

'Uh – just thinking Ma'am. It's nothing that I'm free to talk about.'

The girl looked across at him sharply. 'Y'know, when a man thinks that long, it's just one of two things he's got on his mind Mister Sherman.' She paused just to satisfy herself she had his interest. 'Either he's all set to earn himself a quick profit or he's got some woman problem.'

Steve laughed. 'I can assure you Ma'am that a quick profit means nothing to me and I'd be riding into the skyline long before any woman became a problem, so it looks like there's a third thing that men think on that you haven't got around to yet.'

Myra said nothing. Looking at his superb physique and handsome profile she concluded he must have ridden into the skyline away from many a disappointed woman. She allowed the reserve to build up again and caused her mount to drop back a little. She had no intention of letting herself get interested in the lawman. When he ultimately left town she wanted to be in a position to have no thoughts on the subject.

They rode on in silence for the rest of the way and it was just as they rounded the shoulder of a small hill a short distance south of Blundell when the staccato gunshots split the night air.

Without thinking Myra sent her mount speeding towards Main Street. Something told her that the gunshots held some great significance for her and the premonition caused a sinking feeling to gnaw at her stomach, making her urge her horse to greater efforts.

Steve scratched his head in perplexity as she swept past him, then he gigged the pinto into a run so that they entered Main Street together. They drew up outside Maxim's as the batwing doors were held open and a couple of punchers stepped out carrying a limp form between them. A crowd of men spilled out in their wake. Enough light shone from Maxim's and the dance hall next door to show up the limp form as Sheriff John Dean, and Sheriff Dean was dead, exceedingly dead.

Myra slid to the ground and rushed to the little cortege. The bearers stopped uncertainly as she stood, white-faced and aghast, looking down at her father's body. The great gash in his chest, out of which the blood had ceased to flow, made questions unnecessary and she stepped back. The bearers carried on their way to the funeral parlour and slowly

77

Myra followed them.

Tethering the pinto and Myra's bay mare to the hitch rail, Steve stepped up on to the sidewalk and through the wide open doors into Maxim's. Through the low lying smoke haze he saw the central bar positions taken up by Abe Marsh, Fallon, Hart, Moody and Kurt Munro. Their eyes fastened upon him and Moody edged behind Munro as Steve walked deliberately down the narrow aisle to the bar. He stopped in front of Marshal Hart but just far enough away from him so that Marsh and his cronies were still in view.

'For a lawman you don't seem to be taking much interest in the killing that just took place. What happened?'

Fallon went to speak but Marsh held up a warning hand. Marshal Hart swallowed hard then took heart, secure in the knowledge that he was backed by some mighty good gun slingers.

'I do my job, Sherman,' he ground out. 'An' I can't see what it's got to do with you.'

'I'm telling you right now what it's got to do with me.' Steve let his eyes range across from Marsh to Munro, meeting cool mocking glances from each man. 'I'm a Deputy United States Marshal and the corpse just carried out from here was Sheriff Dean. I'd expect a Town Marshal to be showing some signs of battle not propping the bar up with his lazy carcass.'

'U.S. Marshal eh?' put in Marsh. He stared hard at Steve and for a moment his eyes showed fear. 'So you reckon that makes you something special?'

Steve ignored the remark, a fact that made the blood suffuse Marsh's face and caused a nerve to flutter at his temple.

'Start talking Hart.' Steve's eyes bored into the man's shifty depths. 'How did Dean get killed?'

'It was an accident an' that's why I'm propping up the bar,' the Marshal growled after clearing his throat a couple of times. 'Dean was loaded with rotgut. He was standing here with me bellyaching about the chore of cleaning up range trouble an' telling me how good he used to be. Then the blamed fool wanted to show how fast he could get to his shooting irons. He was facing the door an' made to draw just as Moody came in. I guess Moody did what is plain good sense. He drew first and put a couple of slugs into Dean's hide. Moody ain't to blame an' that's for sure.'

Steve looked across the line of men again and the mockery was back in their faces. He knew he'd never break that alibi down.

'I reckon I'll have to take that explanation for now Hart,' Steve said slowly. 'But I'm staying right here on this range and I'll want to know a lot more before I'm through.'

Marshal Hart stared back at Steve coolly. It

was a dime to a dollar that Sherman wouldn't start anything in view of the odds that were stacked against him and the confidence oozed back into him.

'You stay as long as you like Sherman,' he growled. 'You'll find things no different from the way you've been told.'

Steve nodded and let his glance rest a moment on Moody. The little gunman edged a bit farther behind Kurt Munro, the flashily dressed rodeo rider, then relaxed when Steve said nothing.

Steve stepped back a pace or two. In the mirror he had seen Val Trent enter the saloon and knowing the Wells Fargo man was mighty fast at sizing up any situation, he abruptly turned his back on Marsh and his cronies in the hope that the opportunity presented to them would precipitate action. The movement of Trent's left hand was like the strike of a rattlesnake and as his gun spat flame Steve turned again to see Moody stagger forward and pitch to the floor, his guns only half clear of their holsters. None of the other men moved but the killer light shone in their red eyes.

'I guess two lawmen in one night was a bit too optimistic,' said Steve quietly. 'I reckoned on Moody trying for a shot in the back and figured this way would settle the account for Sheriff Dean a mite faster than breaking down your alibis.'

Val Trent stood, his guns still smoking, covering the crowd until Steve joined him, then together they went out on to the sidewalk. Myra Dean was untethering her horse from the hitch rail as the two friends reached the roadway. She looked at Steve with scorn on her tense face.

'He's dead,' she said hoarsely. 'My father's dead. All because he felt he had to prove to you how good a lawman he'd been. I hope you're satisfied.'

Val Trent looked at Steve in surprise but the lawman said nothing. They watched the girl spring into the saddle and haul her mount around to ride away out of the range of light.

'Uh – c'mon Val,' Steve grunted at length. 'Let's get these broncs bedded down and find a place for ourselves. I guess she's got plenty cause to be riled.'

'There goes a mighty nice looking gal Steve,' Val muttered as he unhitched his horse. 'You'd better fill me in with the details.'

CHAPTER FIVE

'For Pete's sake get that stiff outa here,' snarled Abe Marsh eyeing Moody's body balefully, and a couple of cowhands who had just stepped away from the comparative safety of an alcove hurried to do his bidding. Marsh turned his back on the scene and reached over the bar for his glass.

'We're gonna have to salivate that Sherman, Abe,' said Fallon as he too turned to the bar. 'And that sidekick of his. They're both fast enough with their guns to cause us a lot of grief.'

'That's where you're wrong Fallon,' grunted Marsh. 'I've been doing some thinking and I reckon it's time to stop bucking the law.' Fallon's eyelids lifted in surprise then slitted as he digested the younger man's remarks. 'We've got Blundell in our pockets and nobody's gonna buck us on the range. The only thing a lawman can do for us now is help us keep what we've got.'

Marshal Hart and Kurt Munro both heard Marsh's remarks. Munro leaned across the bar and eyed Marsh coolly.

'Looks like you're making a big mistake Abe,' he said. 'The way I figure Sherman, he'll make it so's you have to go against him and he won't be satisfied until he's pried you away from everything you've got.'

'Yeah, that's the way I see it too,' put in Hart. 'He's not going to forget that four of your men have tried to gun him down.'

Marsh shrugged and lit a cheroot. He watched the smoke spiralling for a couple of minutes then let his cold eyes rest on them.

'If you two want to fight Sherman then you're welcome. Just let it be known you're not working for me, and don't expect me or any of the others to back your play.' He edged away a bit and motioned Fallon nearer. 'I'm leaving town for the spread Lew,' he said quietly. 'You look after things here and tell the boys to give Sherman all the elbow room he wants. If things stay quiet he'll have to upstake and get to hell outa here.'

Fallon nodded. 'Could be you're right, Abe. If we salivate Sherman there'll be another one here then another until the military move in.'

Marsh moved away from the bar and stopped in front of Marshal Hart.

'If I was in your place I'd be getting that gaol-house cleaned up and doing the rounds.'

He said nothing to Munro as he passed him on the way out and the rodeo rider gazed after Marsh, a thoughtful expression on his face. Munro wasn't tied to Marsh. He had done odd jobs for him and had been paid but that was as far as it went. His momentary preoccupation was not caused through consideration of the relationship between him and Marsh however but because it was the last thing he wanted for Marsh and his men to become law-abiding during Sherman's stay. The more hell that was stirred up the better it suited Kurt Munro, and his fertile mind played around with ways and means to fan the flames. He need not have worried. The fuel was on its way, three thousand cloven-hooved chunks of it; the fuel Steve Sherman realised would be necessary to bring things out into the open.

Abe Marsh saddled up his black gelding and rode out of town unhurriedly. His thoughts were centred on Steve Sherman. Something about Sherman had bothered him right from the beginning but now that the Marshal's identity was out in the open, the name coupled with the man's occupation caused him to think back hard over the years. The name meant something but he was sure he'd never seen the marshal before. Finally he pushed his thoughts away. He decided that Sherman was concerned only in tracing the hold-up men and bringing the range war to a close. Well, the range war was done. Alec Pownall had been the last to resist and the hold-ups he dismissed with a shrug.

He looked back over the years, a tight smile

of satisfaction on his autocratic face. He'd amassed plenty of coin and got himself out of a few tight corners without once seeing the inside of a gaol. He had made fair pickings for a lot of other men too, those who had the gall to back his play, and now was the time for settling down, consolidating his gains. Sherman would be powerless to act against him so long as he made no positive move to obstruct the lawman. The actions of his men to date could be dismissed by the simple fact that they were free to indulge in their own grudge fights. He employed them but he wasn't their keeper. They were dead anyway now.

Marsh had known for a long time the pattern of things for him. He had made a study of small towns; had seen big men moving in and taking over, had observed the final acceptance of the newcomers and the slow withdrawal of the iron hand, the community spirit being re-established with the big man kingpin. He had played the game out in Blundell ruthlessly and now was the time for the mailed fist to go out of sight.

In time his roughneck crew would move on. The restrictions he'd have to impose upon them to effect his acceptance and consolidation would irk them to the point of defection, and rather than go against him they'd head for new pastures. The men he would take on in place of them would be dependable cowhands, loyal and basically honest. His reputation would emerge as a hard but good employer and he'd boss Blundell without conscious effort.

He tugged a cheroot out of his inside pocket and biting off the end, lit up, taking deep contented pulls at it. One chore he'd have to do himself before he'd be able to feel really settled just so that the past couldn't creep up on him and that was to eliminate Lew Fallon. Lew had been close to him throughout the years and knew all about the past and all the time had been content to let Marsh be the boss. He had remained for the most part inscrutable, a killer with a macabre lust for blood. In the past he had instrumented Marsh's plans with a callous enjoyment but always Marsh had nurtured the feeling that Fallon would one day try for the jackpot and attempt to usurp his boss's command.

Marsh ground out the end of his cheroot on his heel and smiled tightly to himself. Maybe if he played his cards, he could get Sherman to do the chore for him. He upped the speed of his mount as he emerged out of a long dry wash on to open grassland and rode on, blissfully unaware that the range war was far from done.

Myra Dean checked the speed of her mount as the south end of Main Street petered out into the dusty El Reno trail. Already she regretted the haste with which she had ridden away from the Marshal and his friend. Now that she was alone under the black sky with the noise of Blundell muted to a whisper, she reflected she had nothing to ride back to El Reno for except the clothing and bits and pieces of furniture that had constituted home. All that had mattered for her in El Reno now lay in the funeral parlour in Blundell.

She wiped the tears away from her face savagely. John Dean had been mother and father to her and his passing was something that would be difficult to accept for a long time. Deep in her heart she knew that Steve Sherman could not be blamed for his death. Her father had ridden in to Blundell of his own free will, no doubt expecting Sherman to be there and to back his play, but she could not help feeling that after stirring up her father's conscience, the Marshal should have been where trouble was liable to break and so by negligence was in part responsible for what had happened. In the midst of her grief she knew she hated Steve Sherman for having caused her world to tumble around her.

So burned up was she that she didn't notice the signs her mount gave that another rider was approaching and she came face to face with the oncoming horse and man before she realised. It was with a long sigh of relief that she recognised Tom Digby. He hauled his horse to a stop and stretched out a hand to hold her.

'Hey Miss Myra, this is no time for you to be riding this trail,' he said. 'What in heck makes it necessary for you to be riding this time of night?'

She had known Digby a long time and although she had never thought about him one way or another the fact that he was of her father's generation enabled her to release the flood gates. Through her tears she told her story.

Digby's eyes gleamed a little in the pale moonlight as she related that Sherman was a U.S. Marshal, but he said nothing until Myra's voice trailed off.

'I'm plumb sorry for what's happened Miss Myra,' he muttered. 'I reckon your pa was a good friend of mine. Now there's no call for you to ride back to El Reno. You come along with me. Claire will be only too glad of your company.'

Female company at this time was what Myra needed and she nodded her agreement. Digby gave an approving grunt and eased her mount's rein before leading the way back on the Blundell trail. Myra hauled her mare around and rode abreast of Digby as now she felt she wanted company most of all.

Kurt Munro bought a bottle of bourbon and followed Marshal Hart outside. Hart was standing on the sidewalk considering the advice Marsh had thrown at him. Munro touched his shoulder and held the bottle up in front of the man's eyes.

'C'mon, let's split this in the gaolhouse,' he said with a grin. 'Going the rounds is for lawmen.'

'You're blamed right Munro. I reckon Abe's gone plumb loco.'

A few minutes later they sat opposite each other in the gaolhouse. Munro blew the surface dust off the table and filled up the glasses Hart placed in front of him. The Marshal passed a hand over his big face and eyed the younger man searchingly.

'You're a mighty deep bird Munro,' he said. 'D'you think Abe means to give Sherman a free passage in Blundell?'

'Yeah. I reckon so. Abe's reached the point when it'll pay him to side with the law. And one thing for sure, Abe Marsh always knows just where he stands.'

Hart considered this for some time then drained his glass to help his thoughts along. Munro filled it again.

'Kinda leaves you out on a limb,' he put in slyly. 'Looks like it leaves you having to answer all the questions and by the looks of Sherman, he'll be asking an awful lot of questions.'

Hart drank deeply again and gazed doubtfully at the handsome rodeo rider.

'There ain't nothing stopping me from handing this badge in,' he said at length. 'I guess I'll do that come morning.'

Munro shook his head while he poured another drink for both of them.

'Nope, I don't think Marsh would like that. Maybe he doesn't want to fight Sherman but he'd like you on hand to check on his moves. Not that Sherman would tell you much. You've gotta face it. I don't think he rates you high for a lawman.'

Hart snorted and reached for his glass again.

'One way and another your future's looking mighty grim,' went on Munro remorselessly.

Hart shook his head vehemently. 'Nope, I reckon Abe will look after things like he's always done,' he ground out. 'He's called the tune as long as I've known him.' He took another drink and stared into the middle distance for a long time. When he brought his eyes back to Munro the doubt was back on his face. 'What's your angle anyway?' he asked. 'Blamed if I've ever been able to figure you.'

Munro took a sip at his drink and weighed Hart carefully.

'My angle could bring you in a lot of dinero,' he said slowly. 'Enough dinero to hightail wherever you fancy and live it up for the rest of your natural.'

Hart was now all attention. 'Howcome you're letting me in?' he asked.

'Because Moody was blame fool enough to get himself killed,' Munro answered. 'We had things all set up together then he had to try for Sherman's blood just for the hell of it.'

'What's the set-up that's gonna bring in all this dinero?' Hart asked eagerly.

Munro stood up with a short laugh.

'You think things over tonight,' he said quietly. 'Let me know tomorrow that you're with me and I'll let you into the plan.'

Hart watched him go out into the street then reached for the bottle. Before the night was much older he came around to thinking that if Munro had a plan it would be a good one and that he might just as well be on the inside.

Steve Sherman and Val Trent sat on the edge of their bunks in the second rate hotel run by Jasper Dulin and pulled their boots off with grimaces of pleasure. Steve rolled himself a cigarette and tossed the makings across to his friend. Trent caught the sack and made a cigarette expertly with one hand. He cocked an inquisitive eye at Steve.

'How come you turned your back on those jaspers Steve?' he asked. 'They looked a mighty mean bunch to walk away from.'

Steve grinned and drew deeply on his

cigarette before replying.

'I saw you coming in and reckoned you'd have the edge on any of 'em. I guess all considered I was holding the aces. They didn't know one of the fastest gunslingers on the Fargo payroll was backing me.'

Trent was thoughtful. 'I've seen one of 'em before, the flashy dresser standing beside the one who tried ventilating you.'

'That's Munro,' replied Steve. 'I don't know how close he is to Marsh but he seems to be with him most of the time.'

'Yeah, Munro, that's the name. Kurt Munro. I saw him a couple of times down in Austin at the rodeo. He hogged the rough riding prizes each time.'

'Must be a mighty good reason for him to be hanging around Blundell then if he can pick up easy money riding. Most riders keep going the rounds.' Steve stubbed the end of his cigarette out and levered his long legs on to the bunk. 'He's a mighty cool hombre,' he added. 'Doesn't say much but it's not because he's not thinking.'

Trent didn't add anything so Steve changed the subject. 'You found the Lazy Y Val?'

'Yeah. I saw the Pownalls. They hadn't been able to bring themselves to leave. Said that tomorrow would do.'

Steve nodded. 'That youngster sure is spunky. He'd like fine to stay and fight it out.'

'That's the opinion I formed,' agreed Val.

'Anyway, I told 'em what we intended doing and right away Mrs Pownall said she'd stay on. She reckoned that she'd enjoy cooking for the outfit. Young Dave is sure bucked too that you're using the Lazy Y to fight back from.' Trent lay down on his bunk, then as a thought struck him raised himself again to look at his pardner.

'Say, I forgot to ask. Did Li Hammond decide to run his herd on to the Lazy Y?'

'Sure, relax,' replied Steve. 'He's got a mighty hard looking crew too. You didn't tell me he had Mike Ringold for scout.'

Trent puckered his brows. 'You mean Mike Ringold who was Sheriff of Tucson until a couple of years back?' And when Steve grunted an assent, 'I didn't see Ringold but he's a good man to have siding you in any fracas.'

They relapsed into silence and within minutes both were asleep.

CHAPTER SIX

The sun had been clear of the horizon a couple of hours before Steve and Val Trent hauled themselves out of their bunks. They were in no hurry and took their time sluicing down at the hand pump set in the yard behind the hotel. Down at the chop house they breakfasted in leisurely fashion and took time out to smoke a couple of cigarettes as they drank copious cups of coffee.

'I'd sure like to ride along with you and see how Marsh's men take to a trail herd crowding them,' said Trent as they eventually emerged on to the sidewalk. But I've gotta take a looksee at the trail from here to Mochita.'

'I guess you've gotta do what Wells Fargo pays you for Val,' Steve replied with a grin. 'But I don't think you'll miss anything. I'm not expecting the fur to fly until Marsh gets the impression Hammond's there to stay.'

'Maybe you're right.' Trent's attention wandered and Steve followed his gaze to where Claire Digby and Myra Dean were stepping down from the sidewalk just outside the Staging Depot accompanied by Tom Digby who was chewing a straw.

'Phew, a mighty fine looking pair of women there,' Val muttered.

Both girls were dressed in neat riding habits, their colouring contrasting to form a very pleasant picture, and Steve nodded his agreement readily.

'I guess Miss Dean thought better of riding alone to El Reno,' he said. 'Maybe she's not so headstrong after all.'

There was nothing to choose between the splendid figures of the girls but the elfin quality of Claire Digby's beauty made Steve concentrate his attention on her and when he saw Kurt Munro detach himself from a group of men standing outside a hardware store and cross to the girls, he felt a surge of temper rise in him. Munro raised his hat with easy grace and after including Myra Dean and Digby in his greeting, devoted himself undividedly to Claire Digby.

Steve studied Munro afresh. The man was tall, well-knit and had the grace of movement of a mountain lion. He had to admit when the man stood in profile that any girl could be forgiven for finding Munro attractive company.

Oddly enough, Tom Digby didn't seem to mind the attention Munro paid to his daughter. Steve would have thought that any of Marsh's hangers-on would have found no favour with the stage-coach owner. Maybe Munro wasn't tied up with Marsh after all. But if that were so, what was his angle in Blundell?

Tom Digby and Myra Dean walked on, leaving Claire and Munro talking, and when Digby caught sight of the two friends he waved a greeting.

'Hiya Sherman!'

He came to the sidewalk and the pards stepped down. Myra Dean gave Steve a cold look then averted her face. Steve's mouth set in a hard line and he ignored her.

'I guess I know why you didn't want to take the job I offered your Sherman,' Digby said, shifting the straw he chewed from one side of his mouth to the other. 'I heard you already gotta job.'

'Yeah, that's right. I couldn't go tying myself down to a schedule.' Steve paused then turned to Val. 'This is Tom Digby. He runs the stage from El Reno to Mochita. Val Trent's a sidekick of mine,' he added for Digby's benefit.

'I don't run a stage any more,' replied Digby, shaking hands with Trent. 'I didn't get any more time. Wells Fargo'll be running through here from now. I guess I'll be packing up and going East before much longer.'

'That's up to you I guess,' replied Steve. 'Now me, I just couldn't get used to life back East.'

'No, I'm sure you couldn't,' Myra Dean burst in. 'Not enough violence and sudden death back East for your liking.'

The look of distress on her face stopped the ready retort that sprung to Steve's lips but his mouth straightened into a tight line and his eyes snapped fire. In that moment Myra saw him as he really was, a straight, clean limbed lawman, a man who would follow his duty through to the bitter end. She regretted her outburst but couldn't find the means or the words to mitigate her remarks. She could only turn on her heels and walk away.

'I guess she's mighty cut up about her old man,' said Digby, removing the straw from his mouth and selecting another from his inside pocket. 'It'll be some time before she sees things straight.'

Steve nodded and turned away. Val Trent followed him after casting a long look at the upright figure of the girl stalking along the dusty road.

'She sure enough hates your guts Steve,' he said.

'Yeah, but I guess she thought a whole lot of her father, and the way she sees it, if I hadn't happened along, her old man would still be chairbound playing out time to retiring.' Steve blew his cheeks out in annoyance and together they walked to the livery stable to collect their mounts.

Shortly afterwards they separated just north of town, Trent following the Mochita trail and Steve heading for the Lazy Y.

Kurt Munro watched Steve and Val Trent stroll towards the livery stable. He grinned at Claire Digby and nodded in the direction of the two men.

'I've gotta notion that Sherman's taken a shine to you,' he said. 'I'm not surprised about that mind, I guess any man with two good eyes couldn't fail to fancy you.'

Claire Digby laughed. She liked Munro's cool effrontery and the masterful way he monopolised her. There was something in her make-up that reached out to him and he was well aware of the fact.

'And what am I supposed to do about Sherman?' she asked.

An air of seriousness spread over Munro's face.

'I'm mighty interested in knowing at any given time just what Sherman is about. I reckon a girl as smart as you could find out.'

She flashed him a questioning look. 'You just tell me why I should help you.'

The smile that spread over his handsome face sent her blood racing.

'When I leave this territory, I'm taking you along. It's your choice whether you marry me or not and I intend taking enough dinero to keep you in spending money for keeps. That's why you should help me now.'

The red blood darkened her face as she weighed his remarks but the main cause was the excitement that welled up in her. The thought ran through her mind that probably the best way to tie Munro down would be by not marrying him. She cast a look around at the false front buildings, the rickety sidewalk, the dirt road with its ankle deep layer of dust, the woodwork on all sides sunblistered and peeling, and she concluded she'd like fine to ride out from Blundell for keeps with Kurt Munro and money, plenty of money.

98

'If I'm going to help you Kurt, I want to know all the answers. I don't do anything without knowing just what the stake is.'

Munro nodded easily. 'I guess that's fair enough but I'm doing no more talking here. Get your cayuse and we'll ride out of town apiece.'

Claire nodded and gave him a long meaning look before hurrying after her father and Myra Dean who had just gone into the provision store.

Some few minutes after Claire had announced her intention to go riding, Myra left Tom Digby, telling him she was intent upon visiting Ruth Pownall at the Lazy Y. Mrs Pownall had helped Sheriff Dean look after Myra in the early days just after his wife had died and Myra reckoned she ought to know about his death. She knew the trail well enough to the Lazy Y, having travelled it often with her father. It was as hot as Hades and out of consideration to her mount she eased its speed. As she turned off the north trail towards the Lazy Y she noticed Claire Digby and Kurt Munro on the skyline ahead but they were so engrossed in each other that neither looked her way. She headed off the trail and travelled through the tall grass towards the foothills where she knew a fairly easy path would shorten her journey by a few miles.

The wind which was fairly constant in the

vast range country suddenly dropped and the atmosphere became stifling from the torrid heat of the sun. Myra looked overhead and saw the sun, a brassy ball of fire in a sky that had turned leaden. She shivered despite the heat as she realised the portent of the sudden change. She had been in dust storms before and liked the experience less each time. Coming to a quick decision she gigged her horse into top speed and raced for the shelter of an overhang in the foothills. She was doubtful whether she would in fact reach the haven before the storm broke but it was worth a try.

The wind started up again stronger than before and the tall grass bowed deeply before it. Casting a glance behind her Myra saw the almost solid wall of dust that spiralled towards her in the distance and she urged her game mare to its top speed in an attempt to beat the storm.

On the brow of the foothill before Myra, Steve Sherman sat astride his pinto and watched with satisfaction the moving dots in the distance spill on to Lazy Y territory. Li Hammond's trail herd was arriving right on schedule as Ringold had promised. As he noticed the colour of the sun changing to brassy red and the wind falling to less than a whisper he reached around to his saddle roll and extracted his slicker and a hood he had made for himself after having weathered the worst dust storm in years down on the Gila. He put them on and scouted around for the most likely place to shelter then he saw the lone rider cutting across the low ground towards the hills at breakneck speed.

The distant dots were growing into recognisable shapes, moving just in front of the dust wall, then the wall enveloped them. Steve slewed his gaze back to the lone rider again and whistled in surprise as his keen eyes recognised Myra Dean. He pulled at his lower lip doubtfully as he saw the dust bearing down upon her. He reckoned she'd just about make the shelter of the hill and he urged his pinto down the grade to meet her. The velocity of the wind increased, closing the gap rapidly between the girl and the wall of dust and then just before the pall enveloped her, he saw her horse stumble and Myra fall out of the saddle.

Steve knew the dust would be upon him in a matter of seconds and his mind reeled at the prospect for the girl lying below. The herd was headed in her direction and unless the cattle stopped of their own free will to bunch in protection from the storm, they would be upon her in a matter of minutes.

Pinpointing the direction and distance Steve urged his pinto down into the wall of dust. The animal shivered and baulked a few times but Steve forced it on. It was now as black as pitch and the merciless particles found their way through his clothing, stinging and scratching like a swarm of demented wasps. The pinto was surefooted as a deer and despite its inability to see, picked its way unerringly to the low ground. Steve rode on until he judged he had covered about the right amount of distance then he slipped from the saddle, trailing the lead rein under his arm.

It was impossible to see through the swirling dust and it was only by hearing the girl's moan above the sound of the wind that he found her. As it was, he bumped heavily into the solid bulk of her horse before kneeling down beside her.

She was lying face downward and seemed not to have fallen into an awkward position. Under normal circumstances he would have checked for possible broken bones before moving her but there was no time now. Already another sound vied with the wind, the noise of a herd on the move. With as much gentleness as time permitted he picked the girl up and draped her over the pinto's back just in front of the saddle pommel, then grasping the lead rein of her horse, he climbed into his saddle and hauled the pinto around for the hills.

The gathering noise of the approaching herd communicated fear to his horse and the animal needed no bidding to get out of danger. Even with the dust cloud thicker than ever around them and the double load on its back the pinto stretched its stride, snorting in its endeavour to get clear of the mass of beef shambling towards them. Steve felt the animal strike the grade just before the leaders of the herd came abreast of them. He let the horse scramble up the slope until he judged they were removed from danger, then sliding out of the saddle he let the rein of Myra's horse drop and lifted the girl off the pinto and laid her down on the ground.

Groping for his saddle roll he slipped the thonged leather that held it rolled, and shaking out a blanket draped it over the girl. It wouldn't keep out all of the dust but it would help. The wind whipped the blanket about so he lay beside her and held it over her head.

After another ten minutes the pall lifted and Steve could make out the shadowy forms of the horses. Myra groaned a little and stirred beneath the blanket, then as quickly as the storm had started, it cleared. The last swirling dust particles disappeared to the west and the sun shone bright and clear.

Steve pulled off his hood and slicker and blinked the dust out of his eyes. They streamed painfully. He was scratched in a hundred places, dust lay thickly over him, and the two horses standing with heads drooping listlessly were covered with grey alkali, their manes and tails stiff with the clogging dust. As Steve thumped his clothing in an attempt to clean himself up a bit, the blanket was swept away and Myra Dean struggled up to a sitting position. Her fall had given her one advantage. Being unconscious, her eyes had stayed shut throughout the storm and she was able to open them without trouble. She shook her head carefully, then finding the movement wasn't too painful she focused her attention on Steve.

'How're you feeling?' he asked as he stopped banging his clothes and reached into his pocket for his tobacco sack.

'I-I'm all right I guess,' she replied. Memory flooded back to her and she looked first at the drooping horses, her own bay obviously lame, favouring one foreleg in its stance, then down below where she must have fallen and the steers mulling along with riders in the distance on the far flank. She looked back again at Steve, her eyes gleaming through the dirt on her face.

'I fell down there, didn't I?' she asked. Steve nodded. 'Then how did I get here?'

'Just so happened I was heading that way,' Steve said simply. 'I reckoned you'd be better off on higher ground.'

She watched the herd milling below, the dust that had settled thickly on their hides making the animals appear like phantoms. She shuddered and considered the simplicity of Steve's remark. It gave no account of the risk he must have taken with the herd bearing down and the dust enveloping everything. She racked her memory but could not remember the herd. The dust must have hidden them from her view.

Steve Sherman was still the man though who had set her father's conscience alight, sending him to his death, and the dislike she held for the lawman was not to be dispersed by his having saved her life.

'I guess I should say thank you for getting me out of the path of those steers,' she said at length. Her tone was grudging and Steve shrugged as he drew deeply on his cigarette.

'Aw – that was nothing,' he replied tersely. 'As I said, I happened to be on hand.'

He crossed over to her bay mare and examined its left foreleg. Myra struggled to her feet and joined him. There was concern in her eyes and a hint of moisture as she feared the worst.

'She'll be all right I guess after a few days rest.' His tone was more kindly as he noticed the glint of tears. 'You won't be able to ride her though. Where are you heading?'

'The Lazy Y. That's Pownall's spread the other side of these hills.'

'That's where I'm headed for. We can ride double.'

The girl didn't reply but Steve wasn't concerned about that. She had no alternative anyway. He gathered up the blanket and placed it beside his saddle roll after having extracted a brush from it. He unfastened the cinches and unsaddled his pinto, then after brushing the under leather work, set about brushing down his horse. When he was satisfied he resaddled.

'Guess those cinders would irritate a cayuse some,' he murmured more to himself than to Myra. 'No point in doing the same for yours,' he added aloud. 'She won't be carrying any weight.'

Glancing down the grade Steve saw the herd was almost clear. Li Hammond rode at drag with some hands he did not immediately recognise. Come to think of it, he grinned to himself, they'd all need a bath before recognition would be simple. A long way behind Hammond came the wrangler with a cavvy of horses.

'Guess you won't have to ride double after all. I'll go down and borrow a horse from that trail herd.' Steve swung himself into the saddle as he spoke and rode down the grade before she could answer.

Myra watched him ride down and engage one of the men at drag in conversation. The pair seemed to be well acquainted and finally rode back towards the remuda. Shortly afterwards they returned, Steve holding the lead rein of a barrel chested mustang. At the bottom of the grade he parted company with the trail herder who waved a hand in farewell, then rode on up to rejoin the girl.

Wordlessly Steve unsaddled her bay and after cleaning the dust out of the saddle he fitted it to the mustang. He removed the bridle and slipped a lead rope over the bay's head, tying the other end to his saddle cantle. Swinging into the saddle he swivelled to look at the girl.

'You all right to travel now?'

She nodded then grimaced as the movement sent a pain shooting through her head. She climbed into the saddle without any apparent effort and Steve reckoned she had fallen in the luckiest possible manner. She could have broken her neck taking a tumble at such speed.

'That's Lazy Y graze,' Myra said, her curiosity outweighing her lack of desire for conversation with the good-looking lawman. 'You seem to be mighty friendly with the herders down there. Just who's taking over the Pownall's range?'

'Nobody's taking it over. That herd's rolling on to Pownall's range for the simple purpose of making it stay Pownall's. Some buddies of mine who'll push their beef until they're nudging Abe Marsh's herd.' He paused. 'The only way to end a range war is to make it too big for the aggressor to handle.'

The girl's eyes glinted and her mouth curled.

'You seem pretty good at getting other people to do your work for you Mister Sherman.'

A quick reply sprang to Steve's lips but he bit the words back. After shrugging his shoulders and letting his bleak eyes rest on her for a moment he gigged his mount into action. He cut back the speed to suit the lame bay and Myra swept past him on the spirited mustang, flashing him a look of hate as she went by.

All the way to the Pownall's headquarters the girl rode on well ahead but although she tried to keep up her dislike of Steve she found herself thinking of him in kindlier light. He had saved her from possible death and had made light of the risk it had involved so as not to embarrass her. There was an air of quiet resolve about him that made her doubt whether in fact he did require other people to fight his battles. He was undoubtedly tall, strong and handsome. Concentration upon this latter fact unsettled her causing her to spurn thought for action and she widened the gap by pressing the mustang to greater speed.

When she pulled up in the Lazy Y compound Ruth Pownall was at the door of the ranch-house while Dave was busy fixing a hinge to the corral gate. He crossed over to the girl as she dismounted and took the mustang as she sprang up the steps to seek the motherly comfort of her friend. She sobbed out her story and Ruth Pownall's arm tightened around her shoulders as the tears flooded. Some of the grief the older woman felt herself, for she had known John Dean a long time and had always admired him for being a just and honourable man. When the tears subsided she went to draw Myra inside the house then paused and shading her eyes looked to where Steve had ridden over the skyline.

'That's Steve Sherman isn't it?' she said more to herself and Myra looked at her in surprise.

'It is,' she replied. 'But how do you know him?'

'We met him in town. He saved Dave from a beating and probably worse, then out there he beat three of Abe Marsh's men who were looking for trouble. He's sure some lawman that, and I'm betting on him cleaning this range up. More's the pity he didn't hit this territory before my man was gunned down.'

Myra digested this bit of information and considered the approaching lawman with new interest.

'Dave and I were just about ready to pack up and go East when Sherman's partner, Val Trent, called to say there'd be a trail herd on our graze. It seems the trail boss is a friend of Steve's and he's set on making a stand against

Marsh.' Ruth Pownall paused and shaded her eyes to watch Steve before he went out of sight again behind a fold that backed on to the corral. 'Dave and I decided to stay on and see how things work out. I guess I'd have had to drag Dave away anyhow, soon as he knew Sherman was making a stand.'

'The trail herd's on your territory already,' Myra replied. 'Pushing around the hills down on to the free range. About three thousand head I guess. If it hadn't been for Marshal Sherman I'd have been trampled down by them.'

She went on to tell Ruth Pownall what had happened and the older woman listened with concern on her pleasant face.

'We only got the tail end of the dust storm here,' she said. 'But we could see it was mighty bad to the south. Well, come on in child. I'll fix a bath so you can clean yourself up.'

She hurried away but Myra lingered by the door watching Steve re-emerge alongside the corral and ride into the compound. Dave came out of the stable like a jack rabbit and dashed across to where Steve examined the bay mare's lame leg.

'Hi Steve!' he shouted, hero worship apparent in every line of his features. 'I guess Ma and me are mighty pleased to see you back.'

'Howdy Dave,' Steve answered. The smile

that spread over his dusty face made Myra's heart muscles constrict. She turned hurriedly and rushed after Ruth Pownall.

Together Steve and the youngster saw to the two horses and later Steve sluiced himself down while Dave worked the pump handle enthusiastically. In the bunkhouse they cleaned the dust out of his clothes until when they finally entered the ranch-house the lawman was as spruce as a man who rode the lonely trails could ever hope to be.

Myra Dean stood in front of the big fireplace while the smell of cooking told them Mrs Pownall was busy fixing a meal. The girl herself was dressed back in her range clothes, looking cool and fresh. Just below the line of her luxurious red hair a livid bruise showed on her forehead. She averted her eyes from Steve and turned to welcome Dave.

'That's a mighty nasty bruise you've got there Myra,' Dave exclaimed. 'You take a tumble off that cayuse of yours?'

'Yes, I'm afraid I was pushing her a bit too fast. How is she, by the way?'

'It'll be a few days before you'll ride her again,' the youngster replied. 'But if you're going back into town on that mustang, I'll take good care of her.'

Myra nodded her thanks and turned to face the fireplace. Despite herself her heart pounded as she felt Steve's eyes upon her. Steve stood in the middle of the room irresolute. He searched for his tobacco sack more for something to do rather than because he needed a smoke. The girl's obvious disinclination to talk made him feel shy and ill at ease. It was with relief that he turned to greet Mrs Pownall as she came into the room.

'I'm sure glad to see you again Mister Sherman,' she said with real warmth in her greeting and Steve smiled his pleasure.

'I thought maybe that Trent would have got here too late to stop you from pulling your freight,' he said, taking the seat Ruth Pownall indicated and reaching for the glass of rye she poured out for him. 'It might still be a good idea for you to move into El Reno for a spell while things get sorted out.'

'No.' She gave an emphatic shake of the head. 'If someone's making a fight for the Lazy Y I guess Dave and me are going to stay right here. I just hope that Dave doesn't get in your way.'

Steve's reply was lost through the arrival of two more riders. Dave and Steve crossed to the door when the hoofbeats sounded.

'By heck, that feller's got the gall,' growled Dave. 'He's been mighty close to Abe Marsh and now he thinks he can ride into Lazy Y territory without getting hurt.'

Steve was watching the approaching Claire Digby and Kurt Munro with interest and hardly heard Dave's remark. Even though the girl was caked with alkali the lissom line of her figure sent his pulse racing. The two riders pulled up in front of the ranch-house and Claire Digby's pearl white teeth shone as her lips parted in a smile.

'Lay off him Dave,' Steve said as he gave Claire a welcoming nod. 'We only know he's friendly with Marsh. I haven't heard of him hiring his gun, and anyway, if I'm going to be pushed into a fight with Munro, I want to choose the time.'

Dave stifled his resentment and went outside to take the horses while Steve stood aside as the girl and Munro stepped into the house. The women greeted each other effusively then after Mrs Pownall had indicated the rye to Munro they left to help Claire get cleaned up.

Munro helped himself to a glass and after an appreciative sip looked at Steve.

'That storm was sure something while it lasted,' he said at length. 'I reckon we were lucky being just on the edge of it.' Steve nodded. 'There was a mighty big trail herd running with that storm,' Munro added. 'I reckon the drovers sure had their hands full.'

Steve evinced very little interest in the herd and gave a monosyllabic grunt. Munro didn't press the conversation and turned his attention to the drink before making his way to the compound for a sluice down.

During the meal that later followed conversation was a three-cornered affair. Myra Dean spoke eagerly enough to everyone except Steve while Dave ignored Munro completely. If Steve had been inclined to sulk because of Myra's cool manner, Claire Digby's warmth would have cheered him. She addressed most of her remarks to him and her big brown eyes roved over his muscular frame in a manner calculated to make him aware of the fact. Her animation lent a beauty to her face that completely captivated the lawman and he responded with mounting pleasure.

Myra, remembering the apparent intimacy of Kurt Munro and Claire, watched the extra attentiveness Claire showed to Steve with some surprise. She noticed that Munro had a quiet smile on his face, a sort of semi-indulgent expression. She found herself wondering whether Claire was out to make Munro jealous and felt a momentary pang of pity for Steve. When the meal was finished Munro stood up, waiving the offer of a drink, and smiled his thanks to Mrs Pownall.

'That was a mighty nice meal Ma'am,' he said. 'I'll be riding along now. I guess you'll be riding in with Miss Myra,' he added turning to Claire, and when she took time out of looking at Steve to nod, he made his way out of the house.

There was a slow smile on Munro's face as he rode away shortly after. When the rolling plain hid him from view of the occupants of the Lazy Y, he dismounted and crept up to the brow of the knoll to keep watch. He saw the half dozen or so drovers ride up to the ranch-house some time later and noted the cordial greetings between the tall man who must be the trail boss and Steve Sherman. Shading his eyes he looked to the south for sign of the herd but saw nothing. The answer came to him slowly. So the herd was pushing on to the free range now used exclusively by Abe Marsh. Things were sure working out. He returned to his horse and remounting, headed towards Blundell, a contented expression on his face.

CHAPTER SEVEN

Mike Ringold wiped the sweat and dust from his brow and squinted ahead to where a big bunch of steers grazed. He grinned and turned to his two companions who had ridden with him well ahead of point.

'I guess we've made contact,' he said, his white teeth gleaming. 'They'll have seen our dust by now so I reckon we'll have company mighty soon. Ride back apiece Rod and signal Sloane to get the herd milling. You should be back before the company joins us.'

'You betcha!' Rod was a weedy spavined-looking drover but the steadiness of his eyes showed his spirit ran high. He hauled his bronc around and rode back to where he would be seen by Jed Sloane at point.

'I take it, Mike, that any company coming from the south will be punching cows for Marsh?'

Ringold turned in the saddle and nodded meaningly to the whipcord tough Al Shiels who had been his Deputy down at Tucson.

Shiels checked his guns methodically then eased his position before making a cigarette.

'Here they come Mike!' Shiels nodded to where a few riders emerged from the ruck of cattle to the south and headed towards them.

'Burning leather too,' Ringold commented. 'Rod will have to spur that bronc of his if he's not gonna miss the fun.'

Shiels glanced behind him and grunted. 'Rod's not the one to miss anything. He's on his way back now.'

Ringold smiled but kept his eyes on the riders who had now drawn well way from the herd they'd been guarding. By the time Marsh's men were a hundred yards away Rod had taken his place beside Al Shiels. The riders slowed until just fifteen yards separated them from the drovers. They fanned out a little and the leader came on a few more steps. He was a lean tight-faced man with the slate blue eyes of the born killer.

'You hombres!' he barked. 'Just where do you think you're heading?'

'Who's asking?' Ringold's drawl carried studied insolence and the man's eyes narrowed as he took more careful stock of the drovers.

'I'm Cal Brent,' he snapped. 'And this territory belongs to Abe Marsh who happens to be my boss.'

'You seem to have been fed on the wrong information Brent,' Ringold replied coolly. 'This is free range and there's a trail herd back there that's gonna rest up on it.'

The riders flanking Brent were restless. They seemed eager to reach for their shooting irons. The odds seemed easy enough to them for all the calm of the drovers. Brent too felt that talk was getting him nowhere.

'You just hightail it north pronto Mister.' There was ice in Brent's voice. 'And run those beeves of yours as fast as they'll go.'

Ringold's mouth parted in a grin and he shook his head in a mildly reproving manner.

'Y'know Brent, that mouth of yours could get you to Boot Hill. I guess you're lucky I'm a patient man.'

Brent's expression was incredulous for a brief space of time then the choler started to rise. One of his men sniggered and the sound galvanised him into action. His right hand flew to his holster but he was too late.

His horse reared in fright as he slumped forward with a hole through his forehead.

Ringold's grin was still in place as he eyed the four other men through the smoke that curled up from his gun. Sheils and Rod had .45s in their hands way ahead of Marsh's men who sat stock still in their saddles.

'Some jaspers just gotta grab for their shooting irons,' said Ringold evenly. 'Now me, I'd rather talk.' He paused to let this doubtful information sink in. 'But when I talk I like folk to listen.' He pointed to Brent's body now hanging grotesquely from the saddle. 'I told him this was free range and he was fool enough to fight for what belongs to anybody. I'll tell you hombres again this range is free and if your boss wants to hog it he's got a fight on his hands. Now take that cadaver back to your boss and break the news to him.'

The four punchers said nothing. The nearest to the dead man's horse slipped to the ground and tied the body so that it would ride, then fixed the lead rein to his saddle cantle before remounting and riding back with the others the way they had come. Ringold watched them until they had merged with the cattle dotted on the plains. He smoked a cheroot that smelled like burning leather with placid enjoyment.

'I reckon Marsh's got better hell raisers than those jaspers up his sleeve,' he said at length. 'And I doubt if we'll find things as easy next time.'

Shiels just shrugged while Rod explored his teeth with a shaved match.

'Well, we've gotta know what's going to happen next and there's no better place for knowing than Marsh's headquarters,' Ringold continued while resigned expressions settled on the faces of his two companions. 'You two had better press on and keep an eye on things, but don't tangle with anyone unless you can't help yourselves.'

Ringold smiled to himself as he watched his two sidekicks ride away to the west where beyond the rising ground they would be able to travel a parallel course with Marsh's men whilst keeping out of view. He was confident in their ability to give ample warning of any attack. By tomorrow it wouldn't matter so much. Li Hammond would have sorted out a defence pattern by then. He turned his horse round and headed first to the herd then on to the Lazy Y.

It needed a couple of hours to sundown when he rode into the Lazy Y. He dusted himself down and stepped up to the veranda in his calm unhurried manner. Steve, Li Hammond and Dave Pownall were at the door and a few drovers waved to him from the bunkhouse.

'Hiya Mike,' Li Hammond said. 'Reckon you're ready for some chow.'

'Sure thing,' Ringold answered. He glanced towards Dave Pownall and Hammond edged the youngster forward.

'This is Mike Ringold, Dave,' he said, and to Ringold, 'Meet Dave Pownall, the legal owner of the Lazy Y.'

Ringold grasped the youngster's hand as seriously as he would the hand of a seasoned campaigner, and Dave grew a couple of years in those few seconds.

'Pleased to know you,' said Mike. 'It's sure a nice spread. Reckon you'll have a good herd eating up the graze before much longer.'

'It'll do for a start to get back what's been rustled from it,' Dave replied, and Ringold grinned.

'Well, we made contact Li,' he reported, turning his attention to Hammond and Steve. 'Five hombres came hell for leather when they saw our dust. A feller that called himself Brent did all the talking and when he ran out of breath, started in to use his irons. He was a mite slow and his sidekicks have taken his cadaver back to Marsh with the information that the herd's on the range to stay. Shiels and Rod have pushed on to keep tabs on Marsh.'

Steve grinned at the way Ringold minimised his brush with Marsh's men. The ex-lawman was a man after his own heart. Hammond just nodded. He was used to Ringold.

'D'you think Marsh'll make a move tonight Mike?' Hammond asked.

Ringold shook his head. 'If he's the type of man I take him for, I reckon he'll wait until morning and move in to harangue backed by a strong crew.' He paused and searched for a cheroot. 'But I'm heading back as soon as I've packed some chow away.'

'Come on in,' invited Dave. 'My mother will fix you up with a meal.'

Ringold shook his head. 'Nope, I see Tilson's got the grub stakes going. I'll eat in the bunkhouse.'

He turned on his heel and stepped off the veranda, untethered his horse from the hitchrail and led it away. One of the drovers took the horse from him and he went to the pump for a wash before eating.

Before the others had returned into the house, Claire Digby and Myra Dean emerged on to the veranda. Claire's big brown eyes rested on Steve's face.

'Myra and I should be getting back to town,' she said. 'I guess we'll be real pleased to have company.'

Myra Dean stood aloof and said nothing. She looked as though she would prefer to ride alone.

'Well, I guess there's no reason why I shouldn't ride in,' said Steve. 'I'll be mighty glad to come along.'

The limpid brown eyes lit with pleasure

and Li Hammond grinned as he watched Steve's expression. Dave Pownall broke the spell as he brushed past Steve.

'I'll saddle up your broncs,' he said.

Guiltily Steve turned to Hammond. 'I'll push on from town to where you've rested the herd. I guess I should be there before anything starts up.'

Hammond nodded. 'Be seeing you then. I'll ride with Ringold.'

Kurt Munro rode into Blundell in a self-satisfied manner. It looked as though Marsh would be prodded enough to keep the range war alive and that would give him elbow room to pursue his own line of business. He stabled his horse in the livery barn and made his way to Maxim's.

Tom Digby sat at the table he usually favoured, a bottle of Bourbon in front of him and chewing the inevitable straw. Munro paused a moment in front of him.

'Claire stayed on at the Pownalls,' he said. 'I guess she'll be coming in later with Myra Dean.'

Digby nodded and Munro walked on to the bar where Marshal Hart stood with his back to it. Hart grunted a greeting and Munro nodded to the barkeep who poured out a glass of rye and passed it along the bar.

'You thought about things Hart?' Munro

asked after taking a pull at his drink.

Hart inspected the end of the cigarette he was smoking before replying.

'You goin' against Marsh to get all that dinero you're talking about?' he asked at length.

Munro shook his head.

'In that case I'm right with you.'

If Hart expected any sign of satisfaction to show on Munro's features, he was disappointed. Munro considered the Marshal's reluctance to go against Marsh to have its roots in fear rather than loyalty and he wondered just how much sand the man had. He was silent for a while mulling over the degree of courage he'd require from the marshal, then he smiled easily and turning to the barkeep called up two more drinks.

'We'll drink on it,' he said and Hart reached for his glass, the light of greed already in his eyes. 'I'll let you into things in a coupla days,' Munro continued.

Hart was about to expostulate then caught sight of the younger man's face and changed his mind. The easy-going expression was gone and in its place was the set determined look of a man who would have his way in any company. Hart shuddered involuntarily.

When Lew Fallon emerged from the room behind the bar a couple of minutes later Munro was once more his easy-going self. Fallon walked around to the customers' side and nodded to the barkeep to fill up drinks for the three men. Munro waited for Fallon to get comfortably settled with one foot on the low rail, then carefully watching the man for reaction spilled his news.

'Looks like the battle's gonna start up on the range again,' he said conversationally.

Fallon's hooded eyes were nearly shut. 'Howso?' he asked.

'I just rode in from the Lazy Y,' Munro continued. 'And I saw a trail herd of mebbe three thousand steers being pushed down on to the free range or Marsh's territory. And the way it looks to me is that the trail boss is working on Sherman's orders.'

Fallon drained his drink slowly and pushed his glass back for a refill. He fixed Munro with his penetrating gaze while Hart's Adam's apple slid up and down his throat a few times in nervous apprehension. Hart was an eager enough fighter in the middle of a strong pack but with the opposition stiffening, he had qualms.

'Three thousand head eh?' Fallon mused. 'That's a lot of beef.'

Munro looked at him in surprise. Fallon's reaction wasn't quite what had been expected.

'How do you know the trail boss is in tow with the lawman?' Fallon asked after a while.

'Saw him ride into the Lazy Y. Sherman was there and seeing the way they greeted each other I reckon they've been pards from way back.'

'M-mm, three thousand head,' Fallon mused again. 'I guess that's enough beef to make a range war profitable.'

'By the looks of the crew that's nursing those cows the profit's gonna be pretty hard to get,' Munro replied. 'Somehow I don't think Marsh will take up the fight. I guess he'll play clever and try to ride it until the trail herd pushes on its way. If it does,' he added.

'That Sherman sure means trouble,' put in Hart. 'It's my guess he'll stay on this range until it's too unhealthy for the likes of us.'

'Mebbe you'd like to salivate him,' Munro said with a grin. 'He'll be riding in pretty soon.'

Hart edged away affecting not to have heard and busied himself with building a cigarette, but Fallon's eyelids rose a little higher than usual.

'Howcome you know that?'

'I left a gal at the Lazy Y. Tom Digby's gal. She's making a play for Sherman and I'm betting a dime to a dollar he'll be with her when she comes in.'

Munro watched the lids droop down over Fallon's eyes and with a tight smile he tossed down the rest of his drink and took his leave. Hart wasted little time in following. He wanted no part in any scheme that

Fallon was likely to cook up.

Abe Marsh shaded his eyes and watched the riders coming in from the north. It looked as though Cal Brent's men had left the herd they were guarding and Marsh swore roundly. Then as the riders spread out a little he saw the led horse with the rider slung across the saddle.

Long before the riders came into the compound he had made out the wounded or dead man to be Brent. He bit the end off a cheroot and chewed viciously at it before lighting up but he refused to waste any time or energy on conjecture. He waited, leaning against the new redwood veranda rail until the men pulled their horses to a stop in front of him. Marsh nodded towards Brent's body.

'What happened?' he asked. As he spoke a crowd of men came out of the bunkhouse and gathered round.

The riders looked at each other and by silent accord indicated that the spokesman would be the swarthy man who had led the dead man's horse in. He cleared the alkali out of his throat.

'We ran into trouble boss an' it looks to me as if there's plenty more on the way.'

'Howso?' The question came slowly from Marsh.

'We saw plenty of dust coming up north of

the herd and went to see what was happening. We ran into three hombres riding point of a trail herd. Cal told 'em to turn back north an' get to hell out of it but the jaspers just laughed an' said they were on the range to stay. Said it was free range anyway and no one was going to push 'em off. Well Cal called the tune an' went for his guns. The rest of us were a mite behind him but those three drovers were fast, mighty fast. One of 'em drilled Cal before he'd cleared leather. The rest of us are mighty lucky that they held their fire.'

The look that Marsh gave them indicated he'd have liked it better if their luck hadn't been so good, but he kept his opinion to himself.

'D'you want that we go an' haze that herd away Abe?' asked one of the gathering crowd, a tall, dark-faced man with sideburns.

Marsh shook his head. 'I guess not Slim.' He nodded to the four riders. 'You fellers get Cal Brent buried, and you Slim, ride back with your boys and just keep the trail herd from tempting our steers away. Play it friendly. When the time comes for fighting we'll do it our way. And Slim, see what you can find out about the drovers and let me know muy pronto.'

'Sure thing Abe.'

Slim Conway grinned as he led a group of men away to the corral. He'd had plenty of experience at fighting Marsh style and preferred it that way. Why give the other feller a chance anyway. A man's gotta live to enjoy thieving.

Marsh pushed his way back inside the house and poured himself a stiff drink. He wasn't too worried about a trail herd pushing on to the range. He would have preferred to stick by his intention to quit fighting and enjoy what he had, at least while Sherman was nosing around, but if a bunch of drovers were going to make war then he'd be happy to oblige and shift the onus for the trouble on to them.

He tossed the drink down and thrust the problem out of his mind. Time enough to plan his future action when Slim came back with some information.

CHAPTER EIGHT

On the ride back to Blundell Claire Digby kept up an incessant stream of chatter, directed for the most part at Steve. She rode right beside him and the glances she kept flashing in his direction raised his pulse rate several beats above normal. Myra Dean spoke readily enough when asked for an opinion but she contributed nothing of her own accord. In fact, as they grew nearer to Blundell, she dropped back a little leaving Claire and Steve to enjoy each other's company.

The interest that Claire evinced in Steve's work would have made him wary under normal circumstances but he saw no need for caution with her and talked readily enough.

The sun went down but Steve hardly noticed the heat loss. Now and again their horses were so close that Claire's shapely leg rubbed Steve's and the contact kept his blood at fever heat.

Myra Dean found herself losing her animosity for the Marshal and instead felt sorry for him. Her woman's intuition told her that Claire's animated interest was simulated and that if Steve took it seriously he would receive a jolt to his pride before he was much older. She considered him too earnest a man to suffer such a rebuff and was now beginning to regret having blamed him so readily for her father's death. After hearing Ruth Pownall's story it was evident that the charge she had levelled against him that he found other people to do his work held no element of truth. She remembered too his readiness to forgive her and the fact that he had probably saved her life; by the time the lights of Blundell emerged out of the gloom, she felt positively ashamed.

When they passed the livery stable Myra drew abreast and then forged ahead of Claire and Steve. She drew her borrowed mount to a stop outside Digby's staging depot a few lengths ahead of her companions. The lights from the saloon filtered out into the roadway but some of the stores now in darkness held deep shadows. Her eyes, accustomed to the dark, picked up movement in the doorway of the store next to Digby's and she heard the click of a gun hammer being thumbed back.

Her reaction was immediate. Steve and Claire, now a few yards away, were swathed in dim light and the fear that the gunman was laying for Steve affected her strangely. Her voice surprised her by its intensity.

'Look out Steve!' she screamed then the guns sent stabs of flame spouting out of the shadows.

Myra's warning saved Steve's life. The first bullet that would have gone through his heart took a chunk of flesh out of his side as he hurled himself out of the saddle into the shadows. Then as other bullets bit the dust around him his guns were out and sending a deadly hail of bullets against his attackers.

From both sides of the street the guns roared. He saw Claire haul her mount round and race for the safety of the darkness. He heard a shrill scream as one of his bullets found a mark then he zig-zagged for cover, holstering one gun in order to reload the other.

The ambushers were in deadly earnest. At least four men, a couple on both sides of the street, were keeping up a running fire. He gained the cover of the sidewalk on the opposite side of the street from Digby's and bullets ploughed through the woodwork just in front of him. Then a door opened a few yards away and the light that filtered through framed the two men near to him. The door shut almost immediately but the split second was enough for Steve and he fired rapidly twice before moving deeper into the shadow. There was a dull thud as one of the men fell to the sidewalk and a scurry of footsteps as the other ran off.

There were more shots from the other side of the street but Steve held his fire, intent on moving back nearer to his assailants. One bullet gouged an inch of flesh out of his left upper arm and he bit his lip as the pain waves flashed from the nerve ends to his brain. Another gun opened up and a man fell to the roadway, then the echo of gunfire drifted away and the hurrying footsteps told him the battle was over.

There was a lull as he made his way cautiously back across the street, then the doors opened and men spilled out of the saloons to the sidewalk. Framed in light Myra Dean stood, the gunsmoke still spilling out of the muzzle of her gun.

Men were asking questions and thronging around to check up on the victims but Steve pushed past them and stopped in front of Myra. Before he could thank her she holstered her gun and turning on her heel, pushed open the door of Digby's staging depot and hurried inside. Without hesitation he followed her.

Inside the depot office Tom Digby, the rubicund oldster, turned away from the window and shifted the inevitable straw from one side of his mouth to the other. He eyed Steve and the girl in some surprise.

'Sure some ruckus you got mixed up in,' he volunteered but Steve ignored him and reached out for Myra Dean's shoulder. She turned and looked at him, the momentary pressure of his fingers making the blood run to her face.

'I – I just wanted to thank you for taking a hand out there,' Steve said. 'Things were a mite uncertain until you horned in.'

'I'm glad I was some help,' Myra replied. 'But I hope the man I hit isn't dead.' Her manner, until then stiff, softened as she saw the blood seeping through his clothing. 'Oh, you've been hit! Are you badly hurt?'

Steve shook his head. 'Just a couple of scratches.'

'Mighty deep scratches by the way the blood's flowing,' put in Digby. 'You'd better rest up an' let me get the Doc to look you over.'

Before Steve could answer Claire Digby pushed the door open and rushed in. Her gaze fastened on Steve and for a moment she seemed to have difficulty with her smile then she hurried to his side.

'Oh, I'm so glad you're safe Steve. I was so afraid they would kill you.' Her big brown eyes opened wide. 'Why, you're bleeding. Oh, did they hit you?'

'It's nothing to worry about. I guess it looks worse than it is.' Steve treated her to a smile and Myra Dean turned away with a shrug and walked through the office into the living quarters. She shut the door firmly and relaxed with her back to it. Reaction set in and she trembled from head to toe. She had never fired her gun at anyone before and she was filled with revulsion at the possibility of having a man's blood on her hands. There was an element of bitterness in her mind as she pictured Claire fussing over Steve. It seemed ironic to kill someone in an attempt to save a man for another girl. The implication of the thought struck her and she was sufficiently honest with herself to face up to the truth. She loved Steve Sherman and was jealous of Claire Digby.

The door to the street slammed shut, telling her that Steve had gone back out. Recovering some of her poise, she went on into the dining room to await Claire.

Marshal Hart was in the middle of a crowd on the sidewalk haranguing a couple of punchers to carry a corpse to the funeral parlour and making room for the doctor to examine a man who was bleeding freely from a wound in the chest. The Doc looked up and shook his head as Steve pushed his way through. Hart looked at Steve doubtfully.

'You know any of these rannies Hart?' Steve asked.

'I reckon I've seen 'em around town but I never got to knowin' 'em.'

Steve didn't bother to press him. He wasn't prepared to believe much that Hart might say anyway.

'Where's the other hombre that got hit?' As Steve spoke he looked over the heads of the onlookers to the other side of the street. Lights were on in every front window showing the extent of the raised sidewalk clearly, but no dead or wounded man lay there.

'We got this cadaver from over there,' growled Hart who had watched Steve scrutinise the sidewalk. 'Just layin' 'em together nice an' tidy for the Doc.'

Doc Haydn straightened his portly frame. 'You've got yourself two corpses,' he said, nodding towards the man he'd been attending.

Steve nodded. 'Yeah, I guess no one could lose that much blood and live,' he said.

Doc Haydn grunted and pushed his way out of the crowd. Steve turned to Hart again. Lew Fallon had loomed up beside the Marshal and was looking disinterestedly at the dead men.

'Where did the other hombre go who got winged?'

Hart edged away from Fallon before answering. 'These were the only two. I didn't see any others,' he said.

'Yeah, there was too,' put in Fallon. 'I reckoned it wasn't any of my quarrel so I didn't horn in. I came outa the saloon when the shooting died out an' I saw a feller pick himself up off the roadway an' grab a cayuse. He rode south.'

A few other punchers voiced the fact that they too had seen the man make his getaway. Steve looked hard at Fallon but the man's face held no expression and his hooded lids were down over his eyes.

'You sure you weren't egging 'em on Fallon?' Steve asked slowly.

There was no change of expression in Fallon's face but his voice when he answered was brittle.

'If I'd been laying for you Mister, it'd take more to carry you away than it's taking for those two.' He nodded to the knot of punchers who had started in to tote the dead men away. 'I'd have plumb filled you with lead.'

'Just to be sure you weren't trying to do just that when the shooting was on, turn around slowly and let Hart take your irons. I'd like to inspect 'em.'

Fallon's face was a study as he stared at the gun Steve had eased out while talking. Marshal Hart gulped and watched Fallon anxiously.

'Better do as he says, Lew,' he stammered.

Fallon started to turn slowly.

'And don't reach for that shoulder gun of yours Fallon,' Steve warned. 'Let Hart take it.'

Fallon stiffened but said nothing. He completed his turn and held his hands well away from his guns. The crowd moved away just in case the lead started to fly again and Hart, stepping beside Fallon, eased the guns out gently. He muttered an apology as he reached inside the man's coat to get the shoulder gun.

'Just drop 'em there,' Steve barked nodding to the sidewalk.

Hart did as he was told, placing them at Steve's feet.

'Yours as well Hart,' Steve commanded.

Hart looked up at Steve with hatred in his expression but he complied with consummate care. He had no wish to give any false impressions that might give Sherman itchy fingers.

'That'll do fine. Now get to hell off the

street. That goes for everybody. C'mon, move!'

The authority in Steve's voice had the desired effect. The crowd shuffled away into the saloons and taverns. Fallon and Hart went slowly into Maxim's.

Steve went down on one knee and picked up the guns one at a time. He sniffed at them for the tell-tale cordite smell and grunted his disappointment when each gun proved to be clean. Re-holstering his own gun, he scooped the others up and carried them into Maxim's.

The saloon was crowded with most folk talking excitedly about the shooting fracas, but leaning against the bar Fallon and Hart glared at Steve with malevolent hate. The hubbub stopped as the lawman came a-breast of the first table and every eye was turned on him. He dropped the armful of guns on to the table with a clatter.

'Guess you hombres are in the clear inasmuch as you didn't do any shooting. Just collect your irons nice an' peaceful like if you want to stay healthy.'

There was a tight smile on Fallon's face as he noticed the blood still seeping through the lawman's clothing but he ignored the invitation to collect his guns and turned to face the bar. Hart followed his lead and Steve turned on his heel to push his way through the batwing doors. He heard the noise swell up again as he walked along the sidewalk to Doc Haydn's.

The Doc grunted a welcome to him and nodded to a chair. When Steve sat down, the medico came over to inspect his wounds.

'I guess you'd better strip off to the waist Sherman then I can see what's what.'

Steve stood up and stripped off as required. Haydn surveyed him solemnly as he did so.

'You've sure got a man size job ahead of you Marshal putting this town to rights.'

Steve grinned. 'It looks that way Doc, but while there's folk around like you who want things tidied up the chances should be good. I'll just keep prodding here an' there and sooner or later Blundell will clean itself up.'

Doc Haydn grunted as he looked at Steve's wounds. He wasn't convinced that things would happen so easily.

'It's your lucky day I guess,' he mused. 'Another half an inch with either of the bullets that winged you and you'd have been out of action a long time.'

He dabbed both wounds liberally with a tincture that smarted so much it brought tears to Steve's eyes and a smile flitted across the normally morose features of the medico when he looked up at the lawman.

'Sure got some bite that stuff,' he said. 'But I'm betting it'll make you as good as new in a couple of days.'

Steve's smile was wry. 'I reckon it gets the pain done with in one heap.'

Doc Haydn nodded and busied himself with the bandages.

'You know most of the folk hereabouts Doc. Maybe you've got some opinions that could help me quite a lot.' Steve paused and shifted his position to make the doctor's task more simple. 'I'm not only set on getting things to rights on the range, I want the murderer of another U.S. Marshal.'

The doctor said nothing. He knew there was more to come.

'It sometimes happens that a range war lets the lid off a town and sets some townsfolk off on their own profit-making schemes under cover of the general ruckus. Now in Blundell we've had stage-coach holdups while the lead's been flying between Marsh's men and the small ranchers who tried to keep their claim on the free range. Whoever held up the stage-coach killed a U.S. Marshal and I want the man responsible.'

Doc Haydn finished bandaging and fetched a bottle and two glasses from a cupboard. Pouring a stiff measure in each he handed one to Steve.

'Y'know Sherman, I'd say a lot of folk in Blundell would go the limit for a quick profit provided the blame could be shifted, but mighty few would have the nous to organise holdups. Those with the nous would have put in more groundwork in getting information so as to end up with a real haul. All those fellers got was trouble.' He took a steady pull at his glass before continuing. 'Now Marsh, it's my guess he'd turn his hand to anything for a lot of dinero but he'd know the ante. Just now his concern is beef and cutting Blundell down to his size. I don't think he'd dabble at anything likely to weaken his hand. While there's a lot of crimes charged against him, proving he's doing anything else than staking a share on free range will take some doing.'

Steve considered the doctor's remarks as he struggled back into his clothing.

'Yep. I go along with your opinion of Marsh Doc. Any of his gang you'd say was likely to dabble on their own account?'

'Huh – I've had as little to do with them as possible,' the Doc replied. 'But I'd say that Marsh wields too much power for any of them to risk getting at cross purposes with him. Maybe Fallon. He seems to carry a lot of power and I guess he'd go any way he pleased but he wouldn't hold up a stage unless he knew what he was after.'

Steve drank his rye and set the glass down on the table. 'Well thanks a lot Doc. You've given me plenty to think over.'

'Best of luck Sherman,' Doc called as Steve went into the night.

When Steve untied his pinto from the

hitchrail in front of Maxim's he knew that eyes were watching him, but in apparent innocence he hauled himself into the saddle and headed out of Blundell to the south. He knew quite well that the word would get around that he was trailing the man who Myra Dean had shot and who had escaped. With certainty he pictured Lew Fallon setting out after him. Memorising the terrain ahead he decided upon the most suitable spot and he eased the rein, letting the horse increase its speed.

It was a long time before Myra Dean got off to sleep that night. So much had happened to her so quickly that her thoughts chased around her mind in an alarming circle. Two things were startlingly clear amidst the chaos. Her father was dead and she loved Steve Sherman. Nothing could bring her father back and her manner with Steve made it unlikely she'd be able to get back on a footing of any reasonable understanding, let alone influence him to the point of returning her love.

Sleep when it did come was worried and fitful, for the most part filled with the same dream of her father's funeral which was scheduled for the next day. When she awoke with her room in darkness she thought the dream had distressed her to the point of waking her up but the next slight noise told her that someone moving around downstairs was responsible.

Her room was immediately above the back door which led across the yard to the staging stables and the click of the latch brought her out of bed to the window. A pale light from the moon touched the yard where the solid stable block failed to cast a shadow and Myra had no difficulty in recognising the man standing below as Kurt Munro.

It was with surprise that she saw Claire Digby cross into her line of vision from the doorway beneath and slip eagerly into Munro's waiting arms. They stood together a long time then Claire disengaged herself gently, and holding on to the man's arm led him quietly towards the coach-house. The door closed behind them noiselessly and Myra climbed back into bed, her temples throbbing from the riot of thoughts that punished her mind. She lay awake again, wondering what deep game Claire was playing. There was no doubt that Kurt Munro was Claire's man. There had been an assuredness about their meeting that indicated their relationship quite clearly yet she had gone to endless effort to captivate Steve Sherman. Myra mulled around the problem until an hour later she heard the faint click of the latch as Claire let herself in, then the rustle of the girl's dressing gown as she passed Myra's door into the next room.

The problem defeated Myra. She decided that maybe Claire couldn't hold herself back from any man who took her fancy and if such were the case was more to be pitied than blamed. She toyed for a long time with the idea of making the meeting she had witnessed known to the Marshal, then froze at the idea of making capital out of sneaking. No, he'd have to find out the hard way. The shapes of things in her room were emerging out of the gloom with the first light of day before she dropped back into sleep. Next door, Claire Digby slept with a smile of smug content upon her beautiful face.

CHAPTER NINE

Steve stood beside his horse in the middle of a clump of stunted junipers, his ears straining for the first sounds of the rider he expected, and his eyes staring through the meagre light to the trail just twenty yards away. His pinto, breathing easily beside him, shifted one muffled hoof to a more comfortable position but no sound emerged. Steve had tied down every part of his equipment so that nothing would give his game away.

The pinto picked up the first scent and turned its head to the north. Steve laid a warning hand over its velvet muzzle even though he knew the animal could be trusted to keep quiet. Fallon was far too dangerous an opponent to get the benefit of a warning. Sure enough the horse and rider came into view, unreal and ghostly in the thin light, seeming to glide along the trail without the more laboured locomotion of flesh and blood. Despite his certainty that Fallon would be following, Steve felt the goose pimples rise on his skin. It was not hard to picture Fallon as an assassin.

The trail entered the long run of canyons just in front of Fallon and Steve's mouth stretched into a tight smile of satisfaction as he saw the horse and rider leave the trail to the west. He had guessed right that Fallon would round the hills at speed and cut through one of the countless narrow defiles to lay in wait for him.

He let a couple of minutes to go by, then swinging into the saddle edged his horse out of the juniper clump and across the trail in Fallon's wake.

Steve was a past master in the art of night trailing, while his horse had an inborn instinct for avoiding gopher holes and other traps; so between them they were a formidable threat to any quarry. Fallon however looked to Steve to have a hyper-sensitive sixth sense and in consequence the lawman took no chances at all. Using every fold and rise of the terrain with consummate care he dogged Fallon's trail, never at any time too far away so that the man would be lost beyond the strength of the moonlight, yet never presenting himself in view. Considering the speed of the chase it was a remarkable feat.

They rode for a couple of hours and all the time Fallon kept up the pace. Steve was hard put to keep him in view, in fact he almost missed seeing the horse and rider swing away to the left and merge into the bulk of the mountains. The lawman was about to race the pinto from one hump to another when Fallon's change of direction arrested him. Steve paused a while, peering through the thin light, straining to seek out his quarry but he knew that Fallon had taken the cut through the hills that was intended to bring him into a suitable place for the deed he had in mind.

Steve took no chances getting to the narrow gap that gouged its way to the main El Reno trail. He approached the entrance as though Fallon was waiting there for him. Only when it was evident that no one lurked beside the steep rock walls did he guide the pinto into the velvet darkness.

Years of travelling under the night sky had taught him to keep position by the stars and no matter which way he turned and twisted on a trail his sense of distance from one point to another was close to accuracy. He

145

reckoned that the narrow cut, if it ran straight through the mountain, would be about three miles long, and as his horse picked its silent way over the rock floor he cast his eyes now and again to the stars just to check the direction. Fallon would no doubt have pushed on at speed to get into position and it was imperative that Steve should have some idea of the distance he could travel before arriving at the junction of the canyon and the El Reno trail.

When he judged that only a quarter of a mile separated him from the gap outlet he reined his horse in, and slipping to the ground unhitched his lariat. Leaving the pinto ground-hitched he pressed doggedly forward.

That quarter of a mile proved to be accurate in terms of distance but the time that Steve spent inching forward through the almost impenetrable blackness seemed endless. Although his movements were devoid of sound, his own breathing and pulse beats were magnified in his mind so that he expected at any moment the shot to come from the alerted Fallon. It was therefore with some surprise that he rounded a bend in the cut and saw the main canyon that carried the El Reno–Blundell trail just ten yards distant. The moon that had been blocked by the bulk of the mountain from shining through to where he stood filtered its light eerily on to the wide trail and Steve stopped, flattening himself against the cliff face, hardly daring to breathe and straining his eyes for sight of Fallon.

A couple of big boulders stood out from the rock face and Steve sensed rather than saw Fallon's horse behind the one nearest to him, out of sight of the trail. He lifted his gaze to the gaunt overhang shaped like a primitive carving of a mountain lion but the profile of rock remained unchanged. If Fallon was there, he was keeping as still as the immutable stone around him. Steve studied the cliff carefully, the moon's strength just not enough to give him a clear picture, but he was reasonably certain that a gouged channel ran up from the canyon floor to where the overhang menaced the trail. Fallon just had to be up there.

Steve settled down to wait. Time would drag on and on until at last Fallon would decide that Steve had not after all taken the El Reno trail then he'd come down to his horse and Steve would get him. But things didn't work out that way.

No more than fifteen minutes had dragged away when Steve heard the slow hoofbeats of a horse plodding steadily up the grade towards El Reno. Steve stared hard at the overhang for a sign of Fallon but without success. The sweat started to stand out on his forehead at the thought of someone else running into the ambush prepared for him. He felt impelled to do something to save the unsuspecting rider but he knew that any untoward movement would make him an easy victim for Fallon.

The hoofbeats were now so loud that Steve knew only seconds were left to avert a killing. He was about to come away from the cliff wall to fire a couple of shots towards the overhang when he froze. The rider's identify came to him and a grim smile stretched his lips.

The next couple of seconds hung timeless on the cold night air to be broken by the howl of a coyote and followed by the sharp crack of a rifle shot which reverberated and echoed from the faces of the split canyon. The stab of flame had come from the overhang and Steve saw what looked like an ear of the wind-carved mountain lion rise up. He held the lariat he had brought with him ready and waited as Fallon materialised down the narrow fissure.

Briefly Fallon stood, his rifle held at the ready, staring to where his victim lay. In the last fraction of time before Steve's lariat swooped over him, his sixth sense warned him of danger and he half turned, but Steve pulled hard as the loop settled over the man's arms and Fallon fell heavily to the unyielding ground. He struggled to get his arms free but Steve was beside him in a flash. One look of fierce hatred spilled out of Fallon's eyes before they glazed over as Steve hit him once with the butt of his Colt.

Working with deft speed, Steve tethered Fallon so that he would present no danger when he came to, then the lawman hurried to the inert figure in the middle of the trail. One look was enough to convince him that Fallon's aim had been deadly true. He turned the dead man over and looked at him closely but failed to recognise him. The man had been riding with one arm out of his slicker and Steve noted the blood-soaked neckerchief around the upper arm, and the shirt stiff with coagulated blood. This was the man Myra Dean had winged, her bullet having taken away a chunk of flesh out of his arm and side. Fallon's bullet had gone clear through his heart.

The Marshal searched through the dead man's pockets in the hope of solving his identity but beyond the usual tobacco sack, a thick plug of tobacco and a hefty roll of notes, he unearthed no evidence. The currency, Steve decided, had constituted the pay for the fracas in town.

'Uh, I guess you'd never have thought you'd end up by being gunned down in mistake for me before the night was done,' mused Steve as he picked up the corpse and dragged it towards the horse that stood with resigned stance a few yards away. By the time he had tethered the dead man securely across the saddle and led the animal to where Fallon lay, the killer had regained consciousness. Steve picked up Fallon's rifle and placed it in the saddle boot of the dead man's horse then hauled on Fallon's bonds and kicked him into a standing position. After collecting the killer's horse from behind the big boulder he tied the lead rein of the dead man's horse to the saddle cantle of Fallon's.

Swinging into the saddle and holding on to the end of his lariat, he urged Fallon's mount forward. Fallon stumbled and trotted beside him. A couple of times Fallon fell but Steve hauled him up roughly without a word and pressed on. When he drew rein where his pinto stood, nodding in sleep, Fallon slid wearily to the ground but the Marshal took no notice of him. Sliding out of the saddle, he crossed to the pinto and gave way to the luxury of a cigarette, taking his time to build one that would smoke smoothly. He eyed Fallon throughout the process with calculated unconcern but Fallon just glared back, a hard smile on his face.

Stubbing the spent cigarette out Steve hauled Fallon to his feet and after removing the man's six-guns, bundled him into the saddle. He took care tethering the man so that he could ride easily but still be too restricted to take the initiative. Not that he stood any chance of outgunning Steve.

'Reckon you're cock-a-hoop now Sherman,' Fallon grated as Steve turned away to mount his own horse. 'It's my guess you'll lose some shine when you try keeping me in that hoosegow of yours. I'll be out and gunning for you before you can find a guard.'

'Your gunning days are over Fallon.' Steve's reply was brittle. 'I'm not fool enough to try keeping you in Blundell. You're coming to the Lazy Y until you get the treatment the law prescribes. Considering you just killed a man it's my guess you'll hang.'

'Huh, you've gotta prove that Sherman. It's only your word against mine.' Fallon was unrelenting but there was a trace of doubt in his voice.

Steve didn't bother to answer. He rode alongside Fallon's horse and slapped its rump to get it going then eased aside as the horse carrying the dead man followed when the lead rein tightened.

They rode in complete silence all the way into Blundell. The town was peaceful. Not a chink of light showed from any window and no one stirred as Steve pushed on to Doc Haydn's. Outside the Doc's place he slid to the ground and tethered the horses to the hitch-rail then knocked on the door.

Doc Haydn always slept with one ear cocked and almost before the echo had died away he was at the door. He peered out and grunted as he got the picture.

'Oh, it's you Sherman,' he said. 'What can I do for you?'

'I'd like you to dig out the bullet that killed that jasper,' Steve replied. 'Fallon killed him thinking he had me on the end of his gun. I just want your sayso that the slug you dig out is the same calibre as Fallon uses for that Sharps of his.'

Doc Haydn nodded and went back inside to get into some clothes, then a couple of minutes later helped Steve to carry the corpse inside to his surgery. Steve returned outside and released the bonds that tied Fallon to his horse. He prodded the man inside the house to wait while the Doc attended to his grisly task.

Doc Haydn called out inviting Steve to help himself to a drink and with Fallon's bitter eyes upon him the lawman filled a glass with rye and straddled a chair to enjoy it in comfort. It took about twenty minutes for Doc Haydn to do the job and as soon as he entered the room he poured out a stiff measure of rye to help him forget the chore. He rolled a mis-shapen bullet on to the table in front of Steve.

'Took a bit of getting out,' he said in between sips. 'It was lodged up in the clavicle after having deflected off the breastbone.'

Steve nodded and took a close look at the bullet then handed it back to the Doc.

'That's a .303 Doc, an' that's what Fallon's Sharps takes. Look after it. You'll maybe have to give evidence that you winkled it outa that corpse.'

Doc Haydn dropped the bullet into a drawer in a corner cabinet and locked it.

'I'll be glad to give evidence Sherman. It's time Blundell was rid of vermin like Fallon.'

Fallon said nothing but his eyelids drooped down, hooding the fire that smouldered in his eyes.

'I can put a name to the corpse,' added Haydn. 'He called himself Seth Mullen. He came a couple of days ago to get a tooth pulled. Said he'd ridden up from the Pecos to join his old boss Fallon.'

'That's mighty interesting Doc an' just about ties things up. I guess I'll take the body over to the funeral parlour then push on to the Lazy Y. That's where I'm keeping Fallon until he stands trial.'

'I guess you're right not to try keeping him prisoner here in town,' the Doc replied. 'I'll see to the corpse. You get going so that you're well on the way before sun-up.'

Steve thanked him, and prodding Fallon to his feet pushed him outside and retied him firmly back in the saddle. Doc Haydn waved a farewell from the doorway as Steve remounted his pinto, and taking hold of the other horse's lead rein rode off into the night.

The sun came up when Steve reached the place where he had saved Myra Dean from Li Hammond's trail herd. He reined in his horse and lit a cigarette while he considered things then when he had finished his smoke he headed his pinto south to round the hills. Fallon's eyes lit up as he pictured the lawman riding right into a bunch of Marsh's riders and the acute discomfort his bonds created became more bearable with every mile they travelled. They were still some distance from the point where the hills flattened down to merge with the rolling plain when they saw a throng of riders, two sets of horsemen who faced each other. Fallon's spirits rose as the gap lessened but he was nonplussed by Steve's apparent unconcern.

A few horsemen turned to watch Steve and his prisoner until they were within hailing distance. Li Hammond and Ringold, after a quick glance, returned their attention to Abe Marsh and the few hell-raisers who sat their mounts close behind him. Marsh had transferred his attention to Steve and Fallon and when Steve hauled his tired mount to a stop, the man's eyes fairly bored into him, burning with a hundred questions.

'Hiya Steve,' Li Hammond called, and Ringold flashed a quick smile towards the lawman.

'Howdy fellers,' answered Steve. He looked around and came to the conclusion things were pretty even. Neither side would be likely to start in shooting unless they were goaded.

'Marsh!' Steve's voice was brittle as he edged his mount to the front. 'Is Fallon on your payroll?'

Abe Marsh let his cold glance rest on Steve then on to Fallon. He shrugged his wide shoulders.

'Can't see what business that is of yours,' he answered and Fallon emitted a hard laugh.

'I just want to establish whether he's working on his own account or for you. If you're giving the orders then I'll be taking you in too.'

Marsh said nothing for a long time and the tension mounted. Horses fidgeted but the men were tense and watchful.

'Fallon's on my payroll right enough,' Marsh said at length. 'But I'm not his keeper. I don't know what you're holding him for but whatever it is I guess it's his own affair.'

There were incredulous looks on the faces of some of Marsh's men while others looked downright stormy, but Marsh shrugged his wide shoulders and hauled his gaze away from Fallon's brooding eyes.

'If you're set on keeping this range peaceful Sherman,' he said. 'Just tell these herders not to crowd me. If they're set on staying a while they're welcome but they'd better keep clear of my beef.'

'You ain't got claim to any of this range feller,' put in Ringold in his calculated drawl. 'It's free, an' that says we can push our beef where we like.'

It took considerable effort for Marsh to ignore the invitation to battle that Ringold implied but with deep insight he set about destroying the set-up arranged by Steve and Li Hammond.

'You hear that Sherman?' he asked. 'You just remember if it gets to lead slinging that these jaspers are looking for trouble.' He turned his attention to Mike Ringold who looked back at him, a mocking grin on his swarthy face. 'Just don't push too hard feller or you'll maybe push your way clear to Boot Hill.'

Under other circumstances Mike Ringold would have called the tune right there but out of consideration for Steve he let it slide, as a U.S. Marshal couldn't be seen to side with one or another in a free range quarrel. His job was to end warfare and bring killers to book so Mike contented himself with a snort of derision. Marsh swept the entire trail crew with a frosty glance, then hauling his big black gelding around he rode off south followed by his crew. Fallon watched them go, an odd expression on his face.

Li Hammond and Ringold rode alongside Steve and eyed Fallon curiously.

'What's he done?' asked Hammond.

'He killed one of his own gang who called himself Seth Mullen. I was right there when it happened. Fallon thought he had me on the end of his gun but I guess the law's not interested in who he killed. He'll swing for Seth Mullen just as sure as if he had killed me.'

'What're you gonna do with him then?' asked Ringold.

'Taking him to the Lazy Y. We can keep a guard on him there a darned sight better than in Blundell.' Steve passed a weary hand over his dust-covered face as he spoke and Li Hammond eyed him with concern.

'I reckon you're tuckered up some Steve,' he said. 'Mike and a couple of the boys will take that hombre off your hands while you get some chow at the line shack we've taken over.'

Ringold leaned over and untied the lead rein of Fallon's mount from Steve's cantle, then nodding to his inseparable companions Al Shiels and the weedy looking Rod to follow him, led Fallon away.

'You'd better do like Li said,' Ringold said as he moved off and Steve nodded his thanks.

Hammond set a few of his men to patrol a line so that he'd get plenty of warning if Marsh should make an attack and after instructing the others to get back to their job of wet nursing the herd, he rode alongside Steve towards the line shack.

'That Marsh is a real cagey hombre Steve,' Hammond said after a bit of thought. 'He's well aware that my herd's pushing on this free range to keep the war alive and he knows if he puts out the welcome signs he can stick the blame on us for anything that pops, an' that puts you out on a limb.'

'Aw, I'm not giving two straws for Marsh's virtuous stand,' Steve replied. 'He's caused enough hell on this range and he's gonna answer for it. You can crowd him all you want when I'm not looking. Anyhow it's my bet he'll make a try to spring Fallon.' Steve stopped his pinto after laying a hand on Hammond's arm. 'If I'm not around when Marsh makes a move just see that he's left for me. I want him to myself.'

Li Hammond stared at the lawman in surprise then catching sight of Steve's expression, nodded. 'I'll pass the word around,' he answered briefly and together they gigged their mounts forward again.

Steve stayed at the line shack just long enough to rest his pinto then he took leave of Hammond and headed back to town. He wanted to be back in time to pay his respects to Sheriff Dean. During the return ride weariness spread over him like a cloak and he realised that he'd just have to take time out for a rest or else he'd soften himself up to a degree that would spell danger. To tangle with Marsh's hellions he'd need to be in peak form. He reckoned that his pinto must also be getting near to exhaustion and nursed the animal carefully all the way to Blundell.

When he rode into the livery stable compound the cortege carrying Sheriff Dean's remains was just leaving the funeral parlour.

Steve departed from his usual practice of attending to his mount and handed the chore over to the liveryman. He then set out on foot to catch up with the meagre sprinkling of townsfolk who followed behind the lonely figure in black riding in a buggy driven by Tom Digby. As he passed Dulin's ramshackle hotel, Val Trent came through the door and joined him.

They exchanged greetings and stepped out briskly together. As they made their way down Main Street they eyed the crowd of toughs and loungers who lined the rails along the sidewalk. Sour faces stared back at them but nobody gave signs of having itchy fingers and they passed out of Main Street along the lonely road lined with cotton-woods that led to Boot Hill.

The service was brief, officiated by the part-time preacher whose only interest in the proceedings centred around the fee he'd pick up at the end of it. Myra Dean stood beside the grave white of face but contained. Her weeping was done. The hurt that was left was too deep for tears to salve. As Steve watched her he was filled with sympathy for the girl and at the same time he marvelled at her control.

For a moment their eyes met and in that brief space of time some indefinable spark caused a re-appraisal of each other. A faint smile fleeted across Myra's face and Steve's heart muscles contracted as he smiled encouragement in return.

The preacher intoned the last few words, spilling dust into the grave. Myra stood a long minute looking down then slowly she turned and walked to the buggy. Tom Digby followed her solemnly, the inevitable straw in the corner of his mouth. Steve moved without realising he was doing so and was on hand to help the girl aboard. She gave him a little smile of gratitude that sent his pulse pounding before Digby gathered up the reins and drove off.

'Mighty glad to see you've got around to being friendly with that gal,' Val Trent remarked and Steve turned to face his friend who had followed behind.

'That goes for me too Val,' he replied. 'I reckon there's a few things to tell you so that you'll understand how it's come about. In fact there's a whole lot to tell.'

They waited until all had departed except the grave digger, then walked slowly back to Dulin's hotel. On the way Steve told Trent all that had happened. At the hotel Trent bought a bottle of rye and took it up to Steve's room. Steve sank wearily on to the bed as Trent poured out a couple of drinks.

'Well, it seems to me you've got things nicely on the move Steve,' said Trent after taking a stiff pull from his glass. 'If Li Hammond can stay put long enough for Marsh to show his hand then it's my guess you'll have your chore done.'

Steve rubbed his face, fingering the stubble that sprouted through the alkali.

'Li won't waste time,' he replied. 'He'll prod Marsh into action. There's just one thing that worries me, that I might never be able to fix on the man who gunned down Ellis. I'll just have to hope that he gets what's coming to him amidst the general mayhem.'

Trent lit a cigarette and drew in deeply. His face was thoughtful.

'It's my bet you've got the killer of young Marshal Ellis all sewn up. For my money Fallon was behind the stage hold-ups.'

Doubt still showed on Steve's face and Trent grinned.

'You're never satisfied until you know all the answers,' he went on. 'Now me, I'm ready to take some things for granted or ready to believe that the answer of two and two is four. Fallon's already stepped out of line by going against Marsh and gunning for you. That makes me think he's got worries on his own account. Stage robbery and killing a U.S. Marshal could be the worry.' He paused and drained the rest of his rye. 'Two days from now the stage'll be rolling from El Reno with the Indian pay-off aboard and with Fallon outa the way I've got no worries. After I've seen the dinero handed over at Mochita I'll be back to lend a hand.'

'I hope you're right, Val.' Steve's voice indicated that he had strong doubts. How well-founded those doubts were Trent would never know. The Fargo man shrugged away Steve's remark and tossing down another drink, took his leave.

Steve cleaned himself up and after taking a meal in the Chinese chop house returned to his room and slept until sundown.

CHAPTER TEN

When Steve stepped out on to the sidewalk just after sundown Blundell had a different feel. The light filtered out of the saloons just as on other nights but the hitchrails were practically free of horses and the place was so quiet that the chink of glasses in a nearby saloon sounded like mission bells. One lone puncher walked along the sidewalk lower down the street and his footsteps were echoed back to him.

Hurriedly Steve went from saloon to saloon. In each one just a sprinkling of townsfolk were propped around the bar. In Maxim's and the Gold Strike where floorshows took place most nights, the women were seated dejectedly around tables toying with drinks they had bought out of their own money. He did no more than glance in each place and no one took any notice of him. It seemed pretty obvious to him that Marsh had sent in for the full war party and that meant he intended to take the war to Li Hammond and spring Fallon.

He was about to hurry along to the livery stable when a thought struck him. If the war was going to break out again along the Lazy Y range then it would be no place for Myra Dean, and her friendship with Ruth Pownall made it likely that she would head that way at any time. Without hesitation he stopped at the old stage depot and thumped on the door. A couple of minutes ticked by before the bolts were pulled back then the door opened and Tom Digby stood outlined. He stared up at Steve and shifted his straw from one side of his mouth before speaking.

'Hiya Sherman. What's troubling you?' he asked.

'I'd just like a couple of words with Miss Dean. I guess she's still staying with you?'

Digby stood aside and Steve stepped

through the doorway.

'Yeah, she's still here, staying up in her room for the most part. If you'll wait here I'll get Claire to go and fetch her.' He lit another lamp and pushed through the door into the living quarters.

Steve caught a glimpse of Claire Digby wearing a sheer silk dress standing close to Kurt Munro before the door closed. He was rather surprised to see Munro there but oddly enough he felt no pang of jealousy.

Digby came back through the doorway carrying a glass of rye. He handed it to Steve.

'She'll be down in a coupla minutes. You'd better make yourself comfortable.'

'Thanks, I will,' replied Steve and sat down on the edge of the table. Digby eyed him curiously and chewed away at his straw but Steve took out time to make a cigarette. He didn't feel like sympathising with Digby for losing the stage run and he was sure that Digby would get on to that subject given the opportunity.

It had almost reached the point when good manners would have demanded that he got conversational with Digby when the inner door opened and Myra Dean came through. Tom Digby looked from one to another then with a nod to Steve returned to the living quarters.

The girl was dressed in a long housecoat and her bright red hair had been let down for the night. It glistened and glittered more brightly than the lamp's flame. There was a smile on her face and light in her eyes as she came towards Steve. He gave her an answering smile and held out his hand involuntarily for her to grasp. The contact was electric and they stood for some time, both loth to break the spell.

'I – I've just had a look around town Miss Myra,' Steve stammered. 'It looks like all of Marsh's gunmen have left to join him.' He paused a while to admire the warm flush spreading up from Myra's neck to her face, caused by the pressure he was exerting unintentionally on her fingers. 'The way I see it Marsh will be making a go to drive Hammond's trail herd off Lazy Y territory. Knowing you're friendly with Mrs Pownall I just wanted to be sure you wouldn't be heading that way.'

Myra's heart hammered as she considered the implications of Steve's concern. Looking up into his strong face she found it hard to conceal her feelings for him and for a moment she felt like throwing away all reserve. Her blush deepened as she pulled herself together.

'Thanks for the warning Mister Sherman,' she replied.

'The name's Steve, you used it once remember? When you warned me and probably saved my life. I'd like it fine if you went right on calling me Steve.' He let her hand go slowly, and she nodded, her eyes bright.

'Thank you Steve. I won't go near the Pownall's until you tell me it's safe.'

The way she said his name made it sound sort of special and instinctively he reached for her hand again.

'I'll be riding into El Reno in a day or two,' Myra continued, 'I'm going to collect some things and see to selling the house then I'll be back.'

'I guess that's all right then.' Steve grinned at her and picking up his glass, drank the remaining rye before reaching for his hat and gloves. 'Well, I'll be moseying along.'

Myra said nothing until he got to the door then she ran forward impulsively. He turned and she was in his arms. All reserve went and they clung together a long time before Myra disengaged herself gently.

'Take care Steve,' she said, stepping back. 'Take care.'

He looked at her a long time before replying.

I'll take care Myra but I've still gotta do my job no matter what comes.'

'I know.' Myra's voice was a little unsteady. 'I've lived with a lawman all my life.'

The door closed behind him and Myra held on to the table to steady herself. The excitement of finding her love for Steve Sherman being returned sent most unmaidenly feelings running through her and she had to fight for the control to face Claire Digby on her return to her room.

Out in the street Steve stood a few moments until his heart stopped hammering. His feeling of elation stayed with him though while he collected his pinto from the livery stable and throughout most of his journey to the Lazy Y. As he rode down into the compound past the corrals a sharp command made him rein in.

'Just stay there feller and sing out who you are!'

The voice came from the veranda and Steve grinned as he saw how Li Hammond was taking no chances.

'Sherman – U.S. Marshal,' he shouted.

'C'mon in Sherman.'

Steve rode on up to where the drover leaned his rifle against the veranda rail.

'Go right in,' the man said. 'I'll see to your cayuse. Just tell Li to send someone out to take my place.'

'Thanks.' Steve slid to the ground and handed the lead rein over to the drover. His pinto was led away, and after knocking at the Pownalls' door Steve pushed it open and stepped into the room.

'Why, Steve Sherman, it's good to see you.' Ruth Pownall came forward from the fireplace to welcome him and Dave jumped up from a deep chair by the log fire. Li

Hammond and three of his men were playing cards around the table. They all looked up and nodded a welcome.

'Howdye Ma'am,' said Steve, shaking Mrs Pownall's hand then Dave's. He surveyed Dave gravely. 'The feller you had outside on guard is looking after my cayuse. Mebbe you'd like to take over the chore.'

Dave flushed with pleasure at the easy way Steve selected him for a man's job and without hesitation took a rifle off the wall and hurried outside. Steve turned his attention to Mrs Pownall. 'I reckoned if Dave heard what I've got to say he'd have some fool notion to be riding with us.'

Ruth Pownall gave him a glance mixed with curiosity and gratitude and Hammond and his men stopped playing cards.

'Every one of Marsh's men who ever toted a gun for him has moved out of Blundell,' Steve said, taking hold of the glass Mrs Pownall filled for him. 'They had all gone when I looked around town at sundown. I reckon you know what that means Li?'

Hammond nodded and stood up. 'Yeah, I guess Marsh is going to make a try for the herd, or to drive us off anyway. We'll saddle up.'

'Just give my cayuse time to get a feed and I'll be with you,' Steve said. 'Any more of your men here?'

'Sam Daly's keeping watch on Fallon in

the bunkhouse. I guess he'd better stay and young Dave can take turns to keep guard.'

Mrs Pownall looked anxious now that the range war seemed certain to flare up again on her range. In a short time she had got to know Steve Sherman, Li Hammond and some of his men and she shuddered at the prospect in front of them. It didn't seem right that some of them should lose their lives protecting her property.

'Y'know Steve,' she said. 'I'm thinking I'd rather let Marsh have the Lazy Y than let any of you get hurt. Maybe I was wrong to stay after all.'

The Marshal drained his glass and set it down. His smile was kindly and warmed the heart of the older woman.

'Don't fret on our account Ma'am,' he assured her. 'It's just luck that we're making a stand over the Lazy Y. A stand would have had to be made somewhere if you had gone east so whatever happens no responsibility comes back to you.'

Mrs Pownall wasn't convinced but she appeared to accept the statement. Later standing beside Dave in the doorway, she waved them on their way when they left but she felt heavy of heart.

'I'd sure like to be ridin' with 'em Ma,' Dave said in a wistful voice that made Ruth Pownall thankful for Steve's handling of the situation.

'I guess you would Dave,' she replied. 'But you've got a man size job looking after me.'

He pressed her arm but said nothing.

In the bunkhouse Fallon lay on his side eying Sam Daly carefully. He heard the horsemen ride away and concluded it was likely only Sam Daly and the young Pownall stood between him and freedom.

In between meals they tied both his ankles and arms so that he felt like a trussed fowl but he wasn't unduly worried about that. He had made a couple of tentative tries at getting to the ropes around his ankles and was confident he could deal with them quickly enough. Given time he was sure that he could free his hands. On the other side of the bunkhouse alongside a top bunk one of the windows was broken and a jagged section still remained in the frame. He reckoned that would fill the bill.

Shortly after the riders left Dave Pownall came in to take over from Daly. He crossed over and inspected Fallon's bonds closely before nodding to Daly to leave, then dropped into the bunk nearest the door. Fallon swivelled his head around to watch the youngster and swore under his breath when he saw that Dave was propped up and rolling himself a smoke. He let an hour or so go by then with consummate care started drawing his legs up behind him until he was able to get his cramped fingers to work on the knots. The sweat rolled off him as he strained and pulled at the ropes but he made no sound and Dave remained comfortable on his bunk.

At last the remaining knots gave way to his probing fingers and Fallon inched his legs back to the outstretched position.

'Ain't we gonna eat Pownall?' he asked at length and Dave swung his legs off his bunk to the floor.

'You're hungrier than a timber wolf Fallon,' he growled. 'I guess if things were the other way round, you'd let me go hungry.'

Fallon didn't bother to answer. He knew the youngster's better nature would send him to rustle up some food and sure enough, after stretching lazily a couple of times, Dave went through the door, locking it behind him.

Without hesitation Fallon slid his legs to the ground and staggered across the bunk-house. He made half a dozen unsuccessful attempts to climb on to the top bunk beside the broken window before finally making it. Edging himself gingerly into position he set about rubbing his bonds up and down the sharp window edges.

Time and time again he misjudged the position of the glass and it cut deeply into his wrists causing the blood to run freely, mingling with the sweat that seeped out of every pore. Even though his arms ached intolerably he kept the sawing going with grim determination. When the ropes finally snapped he was almost all in with the effort but he recovered quickly and returning to his bunk, rearranged the ropes to give the appearance of being tied.

A few minutes later the key turned in the door, and after kicking it open Dave entered carrying a tray. He placed it on a bunk and dragged a small table alongside the bunk where Fallon lay. He transferred the tray to the table and glowered at Fallon.

'You can sit up an' I'll feed you,' he growled. 'I'm not untying you tonight.'

'Suits me,' Fallon replied, his eyes almost closed. He made an attempt to sit up and swore as he didn't quite make it. Dave moved closer to help him up then his gasp of surprise was stifled as Fallon's slim hands closed around his throat.

Fallon held on to the youngster when he went limp and only when he was sure the boy was unconscious did he haul him up on to the bunk. He took Dave's gun and gunbelt and slid to the floor. He was about to make his way out of the bunkhouse when the acrid smell of the coffee assailed his nostrils. Calmly he ate the pile of flapjacks that Mrs Pownall had cooked and drained every last drop of coffee, then satisfying himself that Dave would remain unconscious for some time he quickly left the bunkhouse. Crossing to the stable he saddled up his horse and led it outside. Climbing into the saddle he headed south across the compound. He was unhurried, contemptuous of the occupants of the ranch-house, the hoofbeats of his shod horse beating a slow tattoo.

As he drew near to the house the door opened and Sam Daly came through doorway. Daly's eyes were unaccustomed to the gloom and he mistook the rider for Dave Pownall.

'Where in heck are you going Dave?' he yelled as he came to the edge of the veranda.

Fallon fired once and felt savage satisfaction as Daly pitched forward to lie sprawled at the foot of the three steps. He ignored the woman who rushed to the door, and gigged his mount into a trot.

Steve and Li Hammond rode along the line while the night lasted, exchanging words with the men posted here and there to check on any movement on the part of Marsh's men but the night passed without incident and dawn came with two hard-looking crews eyeing each other from a couple of hundred yards distance. Steve scanned the riders for sign of Marsh but he wasn't amongst them.

'Looks like they're waiting for the boss to show up Li,' he said at length.

'Yeah. He's mebbe got sense. Spent the night in bed an' getting outside a mansize feed right now.' Hammond passed a tired hand over his face. 'Let's get down to the lineshack an' get some chow.'

Steve grinned at him and wheeled his pinto around. 'You've sure got me interested,' he replied. 'I don't think anything's gonna pop for a while.'

They rode on down to the lineshack and took time out to eat a good breakfast before returning an hour later to stare at the riders who moved around Marsh's cattle without any real enthusiasm. Another hour or so passed before dust puffs far to the south told them a rider was heading to join Marsh's men at speed. The rider turned out to be Marsh himself.

He rode up to the head of his herd and waved his men in. They were grouped around him for a few minutes then spilled out and to Steve's astonishment rode into position and started to work the cattle towards the south. Steve, Hammond and the drovers looked on as the cattle started moving, stringing out in a manageable line to join up with the rest of Marsh's herd on the more southerly plain. Steve scratched his head in perplexity and Hammond looked at him with a puzzled expression.

'Looks like Marsh is getting smart,' Hammond growled. 'He's not going to fight. He's called his men in to pull freight.'

Steve nodded and searched in his pocket

for his tobacco sack. As he lit his cigarette he saw Marsh turn his horse and head towards them. They waited without any display of interest until he drew rein a few yards from where they sat their horses. Marsh gave them all a mighty bleak look before addressing himself to Steve.

'For a lawman Sherman, you're mighty one-sided. These jaspers drive on the range and start prodding, then instead of keeping the peace, you horn in on their side.' His hard mouth twisted into a sneer. 'I could take care of all the prodding and you along with it Sherman,' he added. 'But I guess the wrong tale would be told an' there'd always be some lawman nosing around trying to fix the blame on me. Well, you can keep the range. I'm heading my herd for Topeka.'

'Run clean out of sand, eh Marsh?' Steve answered. 'You and your roughneck crew were sure some hell-a-milers when the opposition was easy. Now that that lead's starting to come back in your direction, you're wanting away.'

The blood seeped up under the skin on Marsh's face and his eyes glittered with hate but he kept himself under iron control.

'You can think what you like Sherman.' His voice was harsh and he ignored the low laughter that started with Mike Ringold and was taken up by the drovers. 'But I'm heading for Topeka right now because the time is right and the price for my beef will be right.'

He went to shake the rein and get his big gelding moving, then stopped as Steve's voice sounded easily above the laughter.

'You can head where you like Marsh but you'll end by paying for the things you've done on this range. You head out now and a lot of folks are gonna work up the courage to testify against you. I'll give 'em time to elect their own law officers and find a strong enough jury then I'll bring you back to face 'em.'

Marsh sat his mount like a graven image for a long time, staring at Steve with inhuman intensity. The laughter had dried up and even Mike Ringold looked serious.

'You do that Sherman,' Marsh said at last. 'You've sure set yourself a mansize chore.' His handsome features broke into a sneer as he wheeled his horse around and rode away hard, straight-backed and unyielding.

'Waal, I guess that's that,' remarked Li Hammond. 'It looks like we can get going for the Nation. That is, after we've seen him well on his way.'

Steve nodded and Ringold edged his mount up nearer to Hammond.

'I guess you'd like me to keep tabs on 'em until they've cleared the range Li?' he asked and when Hammond agreed, he nodded to his two sidekicks and headed west.

CHAPTER ELEVEN

Fallon had the two large groups of riders under surveillance when the sun cleared the skyline. His horse cropped the grass behind a deep fold on the rising slopes of the foothills to the west of the riders and he lay shading his eyes from the glare of the early sun.

It looked as though Marsh had called in most of his crew and Fallon waited impatiently for the battle to start. He knew he was out on a limb and couldn't join forces with his gang until the war was on. Once the guns started to roar, they'd all be committed and the murder Sherman had witnessed and the killing of Daly back at the Lazy Y wouldn't add up to any more than the general mayhem. He'd take care to settle Sherman's hash anyway.

He watched Marsh join up with his men with satisfaction: it wouldn't be long now. He checked his gun as Marsh's crew went into a huddle then stared in disbelief as the positions they took up indicated the intention to move the herd south. Rage welled up in him as the cattle started to string out. So Marsh was heading for the rail head. There was no doubt in his mind that the herd he and Marsh had thieved from a dozen sources wouldn't stop now until they entered the pens at Topeka.

He watched Marsh ride up to face Sherman and the drovers but had no interest in the proceedings. He knew the answers. So Marsh was leaving him to stew in his own trouble. The sweat started to run down his face as he realised how close he had come to cooking his goose. He had been quite happy to stay a prisoner until the time Marsh would spring him. Had he left it another night he'd have been too late.

Marsh eventually rode away to be swallowed up in the dust the moving steers churned up and Fallon thrust his gun back into its holster. His rage passed away leaving the cold resolve to take care of Sherman first and then Marsh at his leisure.

As the sun crept higher in the sky and shed its molten rays over the range Fallon remained where he was. Sweat poured out of him until he felt dehydrated but he put up with the discomfort just to keep Sherman in view. The drovers below seemed to be waiting for something to happen and made no attempt to move away from the line that had separated the two herds.

A rider whom he recognised as Dave Pownall came from the north and a grim smile etched Fallon's lips as he concluded that the youngster's news was of his own escape. It made no difference that Sherman would know he was at large. He had seen the lawman's gunplay and was convinced he could beat him.

Pownall headed back for the Lazy Y, then when the sun had reached its zenith one of the three riders who had followed Marsh's herd returned. The news he had to tell seemed to give satisfaction and a general lessening of tension was evident. Sherman and Hammond conferred together for a while then when the lawman set his mount to the east, Fallon eased himself away from his vantage point, mounted, and keeping the hump of the foothill between him and the man below, made for the point where he knew he'd be able to ride through the herd without being seen and so get on Sherman's trail.

Steve nodded towards the rider coming up from the south.

'That looks like Ringold, Li,' he said.

'Yeah, that's Ringold all right,' replied Hammond. 'He's taking things easy so I guess Marsh's keeping his herd going.'

The two men lit cigarettes and smoked in silence until Ringold rode up. He wiped the sweat away from his face with his bandana then eased his position in the saddle, resting one hand on the pommel.

'Hiya fellers,' he said, his white teeth gleaming as he grinned. 'That Marsh sure meant every word when he said he was heading out.' Steve and Li Hammond looked at each other with some degree of satisfaction as Ringold continued. 'I got way ahead of Marsh an' saw that the beef on the southern stretch of range had been on the move out before he showed up this morning. Got a good view when the haze cleared a piece through these.' He tapped the field glasses that were slung in their case around the pommel. 'The chuck wagon's way in front of the herd an' headed to cut on to the Topeka trail south of Blundell.'

'Waal, that about ties it up Steve.' Li Hammond shrugged as he spoke. 'I'm real sorry we couldn't prod 'em into fighting but I guess it's the next best thing to move 'em outa the territory.'

Steve leaned over and laid a hand on Hammond's shoulder.

'I'm mighty obliged to you Li for your help, and you Mike. Thanks a lot. I reckon Blundell can start to breathe again now. Mebbe I'll see you fellers on your way back from the Nation.'

'Yeah, I sure hope so Steve.' Hammond held out his hand and Steve shook it warmly. 'We'll rest up today now and head 'em out at sun-up.'

Hammond and Ringold gave a wave as

Steve headed his pinto east. Steve gave them an answering wave and checked the speed of his mount to an easy canter. As he gave himself over to the pleasure of his mount's easy movement he considered the out-of-character action Marsh had taken in leaving the range. He just could not accept the implication that the man had given in without a fight. In a short time Marsh had installed himself in Blundell with a finger in every lucrative pie. It was just not feasible that a single lawman would make him give it all up, unless, and here Steve pondered a long time, unless the name Sherman bothered him from way back.

Steve was only a few miles from Blundell on the trail that ran between two rocky hills when he finally got around to thinking of the size of the gang that Marsh had drawn in to do his trail herding. The man had men in plenty to keep his herd on the trail to Topeka and to make a play against Hammond's herd when it was on the move. He decided to have a look around town in case any of Marsh's men had made their way back in, and then to return to warn Hammond of the danger he suspected and to stay with him until the herd was well on the way to the Nation.

The trail curved just ahead and Steve had a momentary feeling of unease as he surveyed the winding rock face. His pinto's ear-twitching confirmed his fears and he made a hasty check on his side-guns whilst keeping his mount's pace steady. He scanned the cliff tops for sign of an ambusher but nothing moved and he concluded that the danger was at trail level.

He rounded the bend and reined his pinto to a stop as the danger materialised in the uncompromising form of Fallon who stood in front of his cayuse and stared out of slitted eyelids at the lawman.

'Huh! You Fallon!' grunted Steve. He made it sound casual even though the goose pimples were rising on his skin.

The thin line of Fallon's lips broke into a tight mirthless smile and his eyelids rose a fraction showing an evil glitter from each cavity.

'Yeah, it's me Sherman,' he announced in a flat voice. 'Nobody gets clear of me without the score being put right.' He paused searching Steve's face for any hint of fear. 'You've been pretty fast with those irons of yours hereabouts Sherman,' he went on, shifting his stance into a poised, coiled state of readiness. 'Mebbe the fact you're a law officer bothered some folk. Waal, the law don't stack very high with me so you're starting off this time level.'

Steve sat his horse motionless letting the tenseness ooze away from his body. His face showed no sign of the doubt that nibbled at his confidence and the words he uttered hardly reflected the way he felt.

'I've no call to listen to you shooting off your mouth Fallon. If you're gonna draw, go to it, or get out of my way.'

Fallon glared up at Sherman, his face twisted with savagery. He wasn't getting the reaction from the lawman he'd expected. There was a long pause during which the two men stared at each other. Their horses sensed the tension and stood immobile like the ageless background.

The reckoning came with the speed of light. Fallon moved first. His gun cleared leather and was almost bearing on Steve when his interest in life petered out.

The speed of Steve's draw surprised himself. He fired only once and as the gunsmoke cleared he stared at the widening patch of red on Fallon's breast as the man teetered briefly before pitching forward into the dust.

Steve felt no elation as he slid out of the saddle. As always, the uppermost feeling was one of revulsion at having to terminate a man's life. Some lawmen killed for pleasure at the drop of a hat but Steve held human life in such high regard that killing would always be the last resort.

His thoughts made no difference to Fallon. The man was very dead. Steve turned the body over but there was no need for close examination. His aim had been accurate. He lifted the corpse and tied it across the saddle of the dead man's horse, then taking hold of the lead rein remounted and rode on towards Blundell.

The town was still quiet as he rode in. Just a few oldsters cocked rheumy eyes at him as he pressed on down Main Street to the funeral parlour. As he passed the staging depot Tom Digby was unhitching his horse from the rail. He paused and turned to look at Steve.

'Howdye,' he called after shifting the habitual straw from one side of his mouth to the other.

Steve drew rein and returned the greeting as Digby led his horse across to him. Digby allowed his glance to slide to the corpse then back to Steve.

'Fallon eh?' he breathed. There was admiration in his eyes.

'Yeah, Fallon,' agreed Steve in a flat voice.

'Y'know Sherman, Blundell's gonna be a whole lot cleaner with him out of the way. More's the pity I'm pulling out now that you're getting things straightened out.'

'Mm – I guess there's nothing left to keep you here now that Wells Fargo are taking over the run?'

'Nope.' Digby chewed at his straw for a while as though debating what to say then he shrugged his shoulders. 'I'm just riding in to El Reno now to fix the sale of the depot. I reckon if the Fargo men'll pay my price, I'll be pulling my freight in a couple of days.'

'Where will you go?' Steve posed the question out of politeness more than interest.

'Oh, East I guess.' Digby heaved himself into the saddle as he spoke. 'I reckon it'll be a better life for Claire back in the City.' He raised his hand in farewell and gigged his mount into action.

Steve gave him a wave then pushed on to the funeral parlour. A knot of townsfolk gathered there to survey the result of his handiwork but he wasn't inclined to answer their questions and no sooner had the mortician taken over than he pushed through the crowd, fed his horse and made for the Chinese chop house.

He thought about seeing Myra but decided against it as he considered the possibility of retaliatory action by Marsh's gang, and as soon as his horse was sufficiently rested he was back in the saddle headed for the Lazy Y.

The sun was edging over the distant peaks when he reached the foothills that separated him from Li Hammond's herd. Instead of heading through the narrow defile that made a short cut to the Lazy Y south range, he set his pinto to the grade and selecting a fold that hid his horse from the view of the plain, slid out of the saddle and lay full length, scanning the plain over the rim.

The hills to the east were lower than the

level where Steve lay and this fact allowed him to pick up the sign he'd expected. In the brief moment before the sun slid behind the gaunt peaks the haze cleared and for countless miles things stood out in startling clarity. Far away beyond the distant hills the dust puffs rose and spiralled into the sky. He couldn't make out riders but the dust told him enough. A lot of horses were churning it up and that could only mean Marsh's men.

Just before the short dusk gave way to darkness he took stock of the route the riders would take and glancing up at the stars now gaining strength in the sky to fix the position, he stood up and moved down the fold to where his pinto cropped the thin grass. He opened up a can of beans and ate them cold, then after a smoke climbed into the saddle and rode down the hill on to the plain in the line of the distant horsemen.

A couple of hours passed and at last Steve reined his mount to a stop. Unless he had sadly misjudged things the riders should soon be near enough to be heard. His judgement proved sound and only minutes later he laid a warning hand on the pinto's neck as the first muted hoofbeats carried along the wind to where he waited.

He was directly in the path of the riders so he turned his horse away to the north, moving out of the way. Shortly afterwards the huddle of riders swept past him, the sweat of their horse leaving an acrid tang on the night air. With grim satisfaction Steve rode in their wake.

When the gang finally pulled up in a grassy basin on the western edge of the foothills overlooking the Lazy Y ranch, Steve was right there behind them. He heard them dismount and their muttered conversation reached him in muffled undertones. Quietly he turned his horse away to the south and when out of earshot gave it its head. Within an hour he was at the lineshack breaking the news to Li Hammond and Mike Ringold. Before dawn he was back with Ringold and half of the drovers, almost breathing down the necks of Marsh's unsuspecting men.

It was shortly after dawn that Myra Dean finished her breakfast in readiness for her ride into El Reno to gather up her belongings. She was about to leave a note for Claire Digby when the girl came down the stairs already dressed in riding habit. Claire eyed Myra speculatively as she came to the table.

'You're up early,' she remarked as Myra poured a cup of coffee for her.

'I might say that about you,' Myra replied with a smile. 'I intended to leave you a note. I'm going to El Reno to collect my things.'

The cup Claire Digby had just lifted clattered back on the saucer and there was a mixed look of doubt and concern on her beautiful face. The look passed and when Myra glanced up, Claire's face was serene again.

'You'll be coming back of course?'

Myra nodded. 'Tomorrow more than likely,' she replied.

Claire ate a couple of flapjacks while Myra cleared her dishes away but her mind wasn't on food. She was keyed up, waiting for something. She opened the door leading to the old staging office and moved around with her attention focused on the outer door.

As Myra rejoined her in the living-room, horses drew up outside the street door. There was a pause then a knock that sent Claire running to open it. When the door swung open Myra saw the handsome brash Kurt Munro and the two horses tied to the hitchrail, then she understood why Claire was up so bright and early.

Claire returned to the living-room, her face a mixture of eagerness and apprehension. She swept up her gloves and hat from a chair and with no more than a nod to Myra hurried outside where Munro handed her down to the sidewalk and helped her astride her horse. Myra came to the door as they rode out of town to the north. She watched them until the road wound around the livery stable on to the hidden trail. As she turned to go back inside, Marshal Hart rode past going in the direction taken by Munro and Claire. He was unkempt, bleary of eye, and as heavy in the saddle as a sackload of fool's gold.

Myra wasted no time speculating on the association between Claire and Munro. She reckoned Claire was well able to extract only the best for herself out of any situation and equally able to end anything when it suited her book. She took her time getting ready and saddling up her borrowed horse, then about an hour after Claire had departed she headed out of town on the south trail to El Reno.

CHAPTER TWELVE

Val Trent stood aside from the doorway of the Wells Fargo office as Tom Digby came out. Digby glanced at him and shifted his straw to the other side of his mouth.

'Well, I guess that folds it up,' he said.

Trent raised his eyebrows in a query.

'Yeah, I've sold the Blundell depot, lock, stock and barrel. An' I reckon you're welcome to it,' Digby added.

Trent grinned and shrugged his wide shoulders as he watched Digby clamber astride his horse and ride out of El Reno on the northern trail. He rolled himself a cigarette and smoked contentedly as he switched his gaze to the south for sign of the stage he'd be taking on to the Nation.

Right on schedule the dust spiralled in the distance where the trail rounded the shoulder of a foothill. Trent grunted with satisfaction and went inside the depot, pushing through the little gate in the outer office and on into the big room beyond. Jeff Custer, the grey-haired Fargo boss motioned him to a chair.

'Willis is on time Jeff,' Trent said as he lowered his bulk into the chair. 'He'll be here in ten minutes or so.'

Jeff Custer nodded and pushed away some papers he had been working on. 'I guess it's up to you after, Val. I'd have been happier if Willis had been on the Nation run with you but it just didn't work out that way. He had to take the double run south when Chalmers went down with fever.'

Trent glanced through the glass window to the outer office where Peterson, his driver, and Flaxman, the guard, sat waiting. He had known them a long time and was quite happy to be riding with them.

'We've got nothing to worry about Jeff,' he said. 'Peterson and Flaxman'll do me all right. We're lucky that Sherman was moved into the territory. I reckon he's taken care of the hombres who did the hold-ups.'

'I sure hope you're right. Anyway I'll drink

on it,' Custer replied. He poured himself a drink and looked at Trent as he poised the bottle over another glass. Trent shook his head.

'Nope. I guess a clear head will do more good than rye,' he said. Instead he reached across the desk and extracted a cheroot from the box at Custer's elbow. As he lit up the stage-coach thundered along the street and came to a halt outside.

Trent stood up, nodding to Jeff Custer. He pushed into the outer office and followed Peterson and Flaxman outside. Willis and his guard both thickly lined with dust stayed in their places while the three men who were going to take the run to the Nation gave the stage a thorough inspection and the Fargo wrangler unhitched the team before bringing out fresh horses.

The usual crowd gathered to watch the ritual but there were no passengers to liven their interest and one by one they drifted away.

Within ten minutes the stage was on its way leaving Willis and his guard beating the dust out of their clothes before walking stiff-legged into the office in the wake of Jeff Custer.

Trent spread himself comfortably on the wide leather seat facing the direction they were heading. The heat was intolerable inside the coach but at least he reckoned he was more comfortable than Flaxman who travelled on top. Peterson the driver was too busy anyway to notice discomfort.

Under Trent's feet was the false coach bottom. The key that would open it was around Trent's neck. In that hiding place lay the leather satchels holding a fortune in gold coin and currency, the Indian payoff and the eagerly awaited soldiers' pay.

Peterson was a good teamster and kept a steady pace that was just within the strength of his weakest horse. Trent watched the changing pattern of the terrain as they rolled inexorably towards Blundell. Nothing stirred and he began to feel certain that the run to the Nation would be free of incident. A couple of hours passed and when they were just a few miles away from the humped foot-hills where the trail narrowed and ran down through a deep canyon, the stage slowed as Peterson applied the brake chocks. Trent stuck his head out of the window to find out the reason, his six-guns at the ready.

A short way ahead the portly figure of Tom Digby straddled the trail, a rueful look on his cherubic face. He was holding on to the lead rein of his horse. Peterson hauled the leaders back and the stage ground to a stop.

'What's the trouble Digby?' he shouted. Trent cast cautious eyes around but at this point the terrain was pretty flat and it was easy to see that no danger threatened them.

'Blamed cayuse gone lame,' Digby answered, spitting out a straw and selecting another from his waistcoat pocket. 'Reckon it's no more than a strain. He moves right enough except when he's gotta fork my weight.'

Peterson looked overside towards Trent for guidance but Val shrugged any objections away and the driver nodded to Digby.

'Better tie your cayuse to the stage an' climb aboard,' he growled.

Digby grinned his thanks and led his horse around the back of the coach. Trent opened the door for him and a minute later he hauled himself inside and sat down opposite Trent with a deep sigh of relief.

'Guess I'm in no shape for walking in this blamed heat,' he puffed, wiping his face with a big coloured handkerchief.

'Nope, can't say I'd fancy trekking myself,' Val agreed.

'Plumb strange for me riding in a Fargo coach on this stretch,' went on Digby. 'It's kinda funny somehow me gettin' a free ride the first run.'

Trent grinned. 'Mebbe it's not free,' he replied. 'I'll be putting in the report we picked you up. Could be Fargo'll collect from you later.'

'I guess not,' Digby said. 'I'll be movin' on just as soon as we hit Blundell.'

They lapsed into silence with Trent peering

out of the window every now and again. Digby stuck a cigar into his mouth alongside his straw and proceeded to fill the coach with a thick cloud of smoke.

It was just after the stage had started the run down between the humped foothills into the narrowing canyon that the first rifle shot splintered the woodwork above Trent's head. Other shots followed in rapid succession and answering shots came from Flaxman, lying prone on top of the coach.

Trent came to his feet immediately, his guns in hand and Digby struggled off the seat. The firing came from each side of the cliff face near the bottom of the run and the coach would have to run the gauntlet. There was no turning back.

Peterson urged his team on and the stage rocked as the maddened beasts ran at crazy speed. Trent held his fire as they swept nearer to where the marksmen were hidden, his sharp ears picking out the characteristics of three different rifles. He grinned to himself as he looked downtrail and saw no obstacles in their path. Three riflemen wouldn't stop this stage he reflected.

'They're both sides,' yelled Digby, his six-guns in hand. 'I'll take this side.'

Trent grinned at him and nodded then turned his attention to the cliff side. As the coach came abreast of the spot where the riflemen lay, Val emptied one gun at the points of gun flash. Completely absorbed, he didn't see Digby turn away from the window and bring the gun to bear on his back. A sudden stab of pain was all he felt as he passed into Wells Fargo legend.

Digby watched Trent slide to the well of the coach with complete unconcern, then with surprising agility hauled himself up through the open window above the door. Holding on to the luggage rail that ran around the top of the coach, and with his feet on the door frame, he was able to look over the top.

Flaxman was shifting his position to aim at a target he had sighted when Digby's gun roared and blasted his life away.

Peterson drove his team on away past the point of ambush, completely unaware that the battle had gone against him. He was fighting to regain control of his frightened team when Digby clambered on to the top of the coach and came behind him, placing a gun in the back of his neck.

'Just haul 'em to a stop Mister,' Digby said, letting his gun bite deeper into the driver. 'That's if you want to go on living. I couldn't care one way or the other. I reckon I can stop 'em.'

Peterson said nothing but just hauled at his team until they finally came to a fidgety halt.

'Stay right where you are,' Digby growled

as the driver tied the reins to the rail alongside his seat. 'Make one move an' you're buzzard meat.'

The driver turned slowly and ignoring Digby looked at the still form of Flaxman. He gathered too that Trent had been shot in the back.

'Guess you're real proud of yourself Digby,' he said at length. 'You sure enough had this planned right.'

'And then some,' Digby replied. 'And so that the plan keeps sweet all the way we've gotta have no witnesses.'

Peterson moved quickly but Digby's gun roared again and with blood spilling from an artery in the neck the driver fell headfirst into the dust.

Kurt Munro and Hart, the Blundell Marshal, rode up to the spot just as Myra Dean burst in upon the scene from the south trail. Munro's gun pointed unerringly at her breast. The boyishness had gone from his features. He looked what he was; a callous hard-bitten killer.

'Keep coming on,' he snarled as the girl made to swing her mount around. 'And don't try anything or I'll spoil that pretty face with a bullet.'

Myra edged her mount forward to the point that Munro indicated and let her eyes rove around the scene of carnage. Digby rolled down from the driving seat, a big grin on his face. He didn't bother to look at the girl.

'Keep a watch on her Hart,' he said as he made his way to the side door and wrenched it open. 'Give me a hand Kurt. Trent's a mite hefty.'

Munro slid to the ground and between them they dragged Val Trent's body out on to the ground. Digby bent over the dead man and searched until he found the key that Trent had hung around his neck. Without compunction Digby tugged at the cord, breaking it, and with the key in hand entered the coach. Munro was in close attendance. He wanted to see everything that Digby took out of the stage. Honour among thieves was something that Munro doubted.

Myra gave a start of surprise as Claire Digby rode out of an offshoot into the canyon and drew rein alongside the coach. It was enough of a shock to find that Digby was a killer and a thief but to see Claire sitting her horse, unmoved by the evidence of her father's grim handiwork, made Myra's senses reel.

Six bulging leather satchels came out of the false bottom in the well of the coach. Digby and Munro placed two each in the aperejos their mounts carried and two in the saddle panniers Claire had unfastened in readiness.

'Well, I guess that's a pretty neat job,' said

Digby as he unfastened his horse from the back rail of the stage. He gave Munro a significant glance and nodded towards Hart who had his back to them, covering the girl.

'I'll cover the trail while you head on back. Just make that Dean gal understand she'd better play along.'

'You bet,' Munro snarled. 'Anyone not playing along now gets chock full of lead.' A gun slid into his hand and his eyes slitted as he considered the pleasure of the next move.

'Lend a hand Hart,' he called and when the man turned in the saddle to see what needed to be done, Munro allowed him time to appreciate his intention before firing two deadly shots. Munro enjoyed the fleeting looks of surprise, disbelief and fear that were Hart's last worldly impressions.

Myra gazed at Munro in shocked horror as Hart toppled out of the saddle. The man must be a fiend to gun a man down in cold blood. She shuddered a little as she considered her own fate. Munro's mocking face panicked her as he mounted and rode up close. His smoking gun was in line with her breast.

'I've never shot a woman yet,' he said, his voice devoid of emotion. 'I guess it must be something special. Mebbe you'll be my first.' He looked hard at Myra's blouse pulsating with emotion. 'Anyway it's up to you. If you ride along and make it look like we're enjoying the ride you'll keep a whole skin. Make one false move an' I'll fill that blouse of yours with lead. What's it gonna be?'

Myra looked from Munro to Claire. Even in the midst of her panic she noticed that the cold-blooded killing of Hart had made Claire pale-faced and tense but she had no concern for her. The girl deserved to be allied with such a man as Munro.

'I've no choice, have I?' she replied. 'I guess I'll ride along.'

Munro reached across and palmed the ivory-handled revolver Myra carried. He stuck it in his waistband then slapping Myra's mount and pushing its head round, started the ride back to Blundell.

During the journey there was a short while when the two girls rode side by side. Claire Digby looked straight ahead, tight-lipped, but Myra kept flashing accusing glances at her.

'How in heaven did you get mixed up in all this?' Myra asked at length.

Claire Digby's head came round sharply. Greed had taken over her soul and there was a sneer on her face as the words dribbled from her.

'For money of course – money! Do you think I'm going to spend my life grubbing it out in this place? What do I care that a few men have died. What sort of men are they anyway? If they hadn't been killed now they'd end up in a gun fight some place before long.'

Myra gave her a pitying look that only served to enrage Claire further.

'I could work and slave for eternity and never earn one tenth of what I'm carrying here.' She tapped the saddlebags nearest to Myra. 'I don't care how I've got it and I'll kill to keep it.' There was a gleam of madness in her eyes as she stared at Myra with fixed intensity.

Myra divined that a sense of guilt had already gained a foothold in Claire's mind. For all her talk, the knowledge that she had shared in the murder of men for gain had already started to take away the guilt from the possession of riches enough to keep her in luxury for all time. As Munro came alongside Myra turned her face away abruptly and stared straight ahead.

'In a few minutes we're branching off this trail and we'll make a detour before entering Blundell from the north,' he said. 'Just remember, if you make one sign that things are not what they seem, you'll join that old man of yours in Boot Hill.'

The menace in the man's voice made Myra's flesh creep but she showed no fear.

'You'll be coming with us when we go East,' he continued. 'And if you're a sensible girl we might even set you up in business.'

They halted for a while until Digby caught

up with them. His horse was dragging a weighted blanket that served to obliterate most of their trail.

'This is the place,' he growled as he pulled the blanket in. 'Take your time and don't lather those broncs any. I'll ride straight on in now.'

'Sure thing,' grinned Munro as he hauled his mount off the trail. 'C'mon you,' he growled at Myra and they moved off, leaving Digby to remove other traces before riding on into Blundell.

CHAPTER THIRTEEN

When the first hint of light thinned the night's gloom, the sound of cattle on the move came to the men lying in wait above the trail. Li Hammond nudged Steve as movement just below them indicated that Marsh's men were climbing into the saddle. Satisfied that things were going to burst into life the two men slid away from their vantage point and hurried to where Ringold and the drovers waited with the horses.

Quickly daylight took over. They all climbed into the saddle and as the first shots rent the air, rode up the grade then down the other side right behind Marsh's men.

Steve saw Marsh right out in front and he permitted himself a grim smile as he pictured the man's astonishment at the way things were shaping. Hammond's herd had been brought right up to the point where the valley funnelled just below where Marsh waited, then the drovers milled the leaders around, heading the beasts back. While some of the drovers kept the herd going, others turned in a line and sent volley after volley into the ranks of the attackers.

Marsh waved his men on and Steve could tell by the man's crazy behaviour that he knew a trap had been sprung for him. Guns roared from all sides. As Marsh grouped his men, the drovers fanned out to prevent them bursting out of the trap, and Steve, Ringold and Hammond circled and milled, firing into the rustlers' ranks with deadly effect.

Some horses went down amidst the rustlers and panic seemed to overtake the gang. In the dust and gunsmoke Steve saw Marsh, his face working like a demon, trying to stiffen resistance. His shouted oaths had the effect of drawing about six men to follow him and they sent their horses in the wake of the herd, their guns blazing at the line of horsemen strung out in front.

Marsh seemed to bear a charmed life. Three of his companions fell from their saddles but he pressed on after the herd. His guns took toll of two drovers as his horse thundered past them, then he was clear and catching up with the maddened cows. Before the men left behind could take advantage of the path he had opened, they were ringed by Hammond, Ringold and their party. Steve yelled to Hammond as he broke from the ranks and sent his pinto wide on the flank intent on following Marsh.

'It's Marsh for me Li!'

Hammond waved him on and Steve settled down to the chase. The firing died away and Steve guessed that resistance was finished. The range war was done. It just remained to catch up with Marsh. He glanced behind and saw that Hammond and a few more drovers were hot on his heels. He could guess their concern. Already the drumming hooves ahead had increased in tempo and now Marsh and a couple of men started pumping lead into the herd, building up the panic that would send hundreds of tons of blood, bone and sinew into the mad, purposeless helter-skelter of a stampede.

Steve divined Marsh's intention and urged his eager pinto to give him more speed so that he might prevent the man gaining his objective. Already the herd was churning dust that came along with the wind in vast billowing clouds. Soon visibility would be nil. Marsh intended to escape under the cover of the dust.

For a long time Steve was enveloped in thick choking alkali when Marsh was lost to view and it was by pure chance that a shift of wind lifted a patch of dust clear to the herd at the precise moment that Marsh hauled his mount off to the east. The dust cloud settled again but Steve turned left and urged his horse to even greater effort.

Within a couple of minutes he was clear of the herd and Marsh was in full view. Steve eased the pace of his mount; he realised it was going to be a long chase. Marsh was riding a big black stallion that was full of running and Steve reckoned that he'd need a lot of guile to get close to his quarry.

Marsh turned in the saddle once but was content with his lead and didn't bother to use the gun he held in one hand. Steve shook him out of his pose by reaching for the Sharps out of his saddle holster and sending a couple of shots winging past his ears. The man's head slewed round again and Steve saw his legs working as he spurred his stallion on at full speed.

The lawman observed the terrain, trying to guess just where Marsh would try to break through the hills that loomed further away to the east. He didn't want to be too far behind when Marsh made his break. Abe Marsh was clever enough to head for the first cut in the foothills, making Steve change direction to head him off.

This change in direction caused the Marshal to cross a long fold when his quarry was out of sight. Coming up to the rim he swore roundly when he found that Marsh had turned south and had gained a tremendous lead. Spurning further use of his rifle he returned it to the saddle holster and settled down to the task of keeping horse and rider in view. Now and again he cut back his pinto's pace, conserving its strength, and Marsh, now twisting in the saddle often, answered by dropping the speed of his own mount. Throughout the morning they rode, each countering the other's manoeuvres. The sweat steamed off men and horses and it was becoming evident to Steve that the chase could not continue much longer at the existing pace. Time now seemed to favour Marsh. His mount held an undoubted advantage over Steve's pinto. This was the first time the pinto had been outmatched but Steve reflected bitterly there always had to be a first time. It was just bad luck that Marsh owned the horse with the edge.

At last Marsh veered towards the same cut in the hills that Fallon had taken on a previous occasion. Recognising it Steve recalled that it ran clear through the hills to the Blundell–El Reno trail, and gigging his pinto into its faster pace he angled towards the cut, hoping to arrive right on Marsh's heels.

Marsh flung one look over his shoulder and his spurs drew blood along his stallion's flanks. The big black increased the lead with every second and would have carried Marsh out of the lawman's clutches with normal luck, but just when it seemed Marsh would make the entrance to the cut, his horse stumbled, checked, then stumbled again, sending Marsh flying headlong to the ground where he lay inert, face downward, while Steve's pinto thundered up and the lawman slid to the ground, gun in hand.

Marsh didn't move as Steve approached but the Marshal took no chances. With utmost caution he came alongside and stirred the man with his foot. When it was apparent that Marsh was out cold, Steve turned him over. There were no obvious signs of injury and Steve concluded that the force of the fall had stunned the man. The black stallion stood, apparently unhurt after its stumble, with steam rising in clouds from its lathered body.

Taking some rawhide thongs from his saddle-roll Steve tied Marsh's hands in front of him and relieved him of his guns. He rolled himself a smoke to while away the time until the man regained consciousness. He didn't have many minutes to wait. Long before he finished the cigarette he found Marsh's hate-filled eyes upon him.

Ignoring the man he smoked on until at

last he stubbed the smouldering butt out on his heel, then with his gun in hand he gave Marsh his full attention.

'Get to your feet!' he snarled and when Marsh affected not to hear him he stuck his foot purposefully in the man's midriff.

'The choice is yours Marsh,' he said quietly. 'You can either get astride that cayuse or stay where you are with a bullet in your skull.' To lend emphasis to his words he sent a bullet thudding into the ground a hand's breadth from the man's head.

Abe Marsh struggled to his feet, a wild look in his eyes.

'You're calling the tune now I guess Sherman,' he managed to say.

Steve looked at him coldly and nodded towards the stallion.

'Get into the saddle. You're durned right I'm calling the tune. Your day is done.'

Marsh climbed into the saddle with some difficulty and looked to Steve for instructions.

'We'll head through the cut to the El Reno trail,' the Marshal growled as he heaved himself into the saddle. 'Get going!'

Marsh shrugged his shoulders and swivelled round to look at Steve before gigging his horse forward.

'You're making a big mistake Sherman,' he said. 'Hammond's done all the pushing as you well know. All I was doing was giving

207

him a taste of his own medicine. I reckon you're just wasting your time taking me in. Nobody's gonna convict me on account of your sayso.'

'Aw – get going. You make me sick,' snarled Steve. 'I don't aim to have any jury to sit and deliberate on your case.'

Marsh flashed a quick look of alarm at the lawman as his horse moved forward. Steve's face was set in cold stern lines and the first flood of nagging doubts assailed the man.

They rode through the narrow canyon at just above walking pace. In places the walls kept them in the sun's shadow and the wind that funnelled through, although warm, refreshed men and horses. When they eventually emerged on to the Blundell–El Reno trail Marsh, who was in the lead, drew his horse to a stop and stared down, transfixed. Steve palmed a gun and rode up cautiously, half expecting to find aid coming for Marsh from an unexpected quarter. The sight that revealed itself sent a shock through him that held a stab of real pain.

There was no mistaking the blond head of the man who lay face down beside the stage coach and there was no doubt that the man was dead.

As Steve motioned Marsh downtrail he saw the inert body of the guard on top of the coach and when they came alongside, the bodies of the driver and Marshal Hart. The buzzards that circled low had not yet plucked up the courage to ignore the restive team.

'Maybe you'd like to blame me for this too Sherman?' Marsh sneered as Steve slid out of the saddle and knelt beside his friend's body. Steve glared up at him with more than a hint of moisture in his eyes.

'Nope, not this time Marsh. But there was another stage once with a dead man beside the burned-out wreckage, and two more men lying dead in the brush not far away. You think about that one Marsh!'

The colour flooded Marsh's face then as rapidly disappeared, leaving him as pale as death. The lines of his face didn't alter but his eyes were hunted as his mind skimmed the past. He opened his mouth to say something then thought better of it and sat quietly as he watched Steve start in to look for signs.

First glance inside the well of the coach told him that the murderers had got clean away with the money. Glaring up at Marsh he ordered him out of the saddle, then un-hitching his lariat, he tied the man securely to the rail in front of the driver's seat.

Getting up inside the stage he searched carefully for any possible clue but without success. He was equally unlucky looking for signs around the coach. The murderers must even have picked up the shells used in killing the men now lying dead. He regarded the body of Marshal Hart a long time, completely puzzled. He hardly thought that Hart would have lost his life in an attempt to stop a stage hold-up. Far more likely for him to have been in league with the killers. More than likely he'd been shot out of hand to save splitting the haul too widely.

As he scrutinised the ground he searched around in his mind for the names of Hart's sidekicks but beyond Munro he could think of no one else still in circulation. Still he decided Munro would do for a start.

He had noted that Trent had died from a bullet wound in the back at first glance but it was only now as he gazed down at his friend's body that the implication struck him. Val Trent had been killed from inside the stage and by someone he trusted. Once again he climbed inside. Blood stains on the seat and floor confirmed his opinion so he subjected the coach to a further minute examination. He was about to give up when he saw the straw lying in the crevice of the well safe that had contained the money. Picking it up, he climbed down again and looked at it, a thoughtful expression on his face. One end of the straw was well chewed.

Only one man he'd met in this territory chewed straws continually and that was Tom Digby. Digby too would have been trusted by Val Trent. The picture of things became clearer as he considered that Munro, passably friendly with Hart, was thick with Digby's daughter Claire. Digby too would have been reasonably sure when the stage bearing the Indian payoff was likely to leave El Reno.

Pulling his notebook out of his shirt pocket he placed the straw inside the inner pages then got to work lifting the bodies into the coach. It was hard work but at last the four corpses were propped up on the two seats that faced each other inside. Next he tied the pinto and the black stallion to the rear of the coach and slipping the rope that held Marsh to the rail, ordered him up alongside the driver's seat.

Climbing up, Steve took the reins and drove the team down the grade to where the canyon walls widened sufficiently for him to turn, then swinging the team around he headed back for El Reno. During the drive he seethed with anger, some directed against himself. He should have taken a closer look at Tom Digby and Munro, and not presumed that all of the troubles could be laid at Marsh's door. Past experience had shown him that smart men would always take advantage of a range war and he blamed himself for having allowed Val Trent to accept Digby as a friend.

Trent's death was a bad blow to Steve. Although their meetings had been irregular the bond between them had strengthened through the years and the future without those chance meetings held a bleak outlook. Steve swore roundly as he hauled back on the reins when the lead horse tried to dictate the speed, resenting Trent's body being jostled around inside the coach. Of one thing he was sure, there would be no jury, no trial for the men who had perpetrated this outrage. He'd gun them down as cold-bloodedly as they deserved.

Throughout the drive Marsh sat beside him silent and thoughtful but Steve paid no attention to him. Marsh could wait until time would provide the evidence to fix his guilt of a crime for which he too would pay with his life.

At last when El Reno was no more than half a mile distant Steve checked his mad surge of rage. With a shock he found he had been setting himself up as judge, jury and executioner in the way that no U.S. Marshal should; but after calmer thought he still decided to see it through himself and to resign if his conscience troubled him.

He drew the dust-covered stage to a grinding stop outside the Wells Fargo depot just a split second before the astonished Fargo boss Jeff Custer burst out of the door. Men who had been quietly dozing in the shadow rubbed their eyes and lumbered along to see what had brought a stage in off the Blundell run so unexpectedly. Custer needed only one glance to add up to the tragic scene. He looked first at Steve, then coming close, inside the coach. His face was white with anger as Steve climbed down alongside him.

'What happened Sherman?' His voice was quiet. He jerked his head up at Marsh. 'That bustard do this?'

'Nope, not this one,' Steve replied. 'I was bringing Marsh in and came upon the stage. The dead men were strewn around it. It was near enough the same spot where the other hold-ups took place. Looks like they got clear away with whatever Trent was guarding.'

'Must have been a big gang for Val Trent to get himself outgunned,' Custer mused, his mind shying away from all the troubles that would follow when he broke the news down the line.

'Trent didn't get outgunned. He was shot in the back from inside the coach. Who travelled along with him?'

Custer looked at him blankly. Neither he nor Steve noticed the gathering crowd.

'There were no passengers Sherman, an' I don't think Trent would have given a lift to anyone he didn't know.'

'Anyone leave town for Blundell before the stage left?'

'I wouldn't know. I'll ask around, might get a lead that way.'

Steve nodded and the two men organised the willing crowd to carry the dead men to the funeral parlour. While Custer went to check on Val Trent's belongings, Steve hurried Marsh along to the gaol. The Fargo wrangler took care of the pinto and Marsh's horse along with the team.

With Marsh locked up in a cell Steve returned to the Wells Fargo depot where he was rejoined shortly after by Jeff Custer. The latter's iron grey hair had seemed to whiten during the past half hour.

'The only man who was seen to head out for Blundell this morning was Tom Digby,' he reported. 'So I guess you can rule him out an' that only leaves us with guesswork.' He passed his hand wearily over his face. 'Well, I guess I'd better get the news passed along. There's sure gonna be some palaverin' done over this.'

He went to the cupboard and came back with a bottle of rye and two glasses. He filled two big measures and passed one to Steve who downed it in one go, hardly cutting a channel in the dust that caked his throat. The Fargo man refilled the glass with a sort of reflex action. He was too dazed for coherent thought or action.

'Don't be in too much of a hurry to spread the news Custer,' Steve said at length. 'Nothing's gonna bring Trent back but I think I'm gonna get even with the hombre who killed him muy pronto and I reckon the stage'll run in a day or so carrying all that Val died trying to guard.'

Custer stared at him in surprise and was even more surprised when Steve thrust a key into his hand.

'That's the key of the pokey and I want you to be responsible for keeping Marsh a prisoner until I get back. See that he gets fed but don't let him shave. I've got my reasons but don't ask questions. And I'll want a fresh mount if you can fix it.'

'Look Sherman, let some other jasper look after Marsh. I'd rather ride with you if you really think you'll be coming up with Trent's killer. He was a pard of mine too, you know.'

'Yeah, I know, but Marsh is as important to me as the hombre who killed Trent. I've just gotta be sure I can rely on someone to keep him, and that leaves you.'

Custer nodded, swallowing his disappointment. 'I guess Val would've liked for you to ride that albino of his,' he said. 'I'll tell Hogan you'll be wanting her.'

'Thanks. I'll be ready just as soon as I've packed a meal away.'

Steve took his time over eating and permitted himself the luxury of a bath before leaving. He reasoned that no hasty moves would be made by the stage robbers. To keep clear of suspicion they would have to go about things normally for a day or two, so it was nearly sunset before he headed back towards Blundell astride the beautifully built albino mare that had been Val Trent's most treasured possession.

CHAPTER FOURTEEN

Blundell was strangely quiet when Steve guided the albino into Main Street. It was apparent the tough element had moved out. Light streamed out of every saloon and pianos strummed out lively tunes but the hum of human conversation was conspicuously absent. He rode straight on through to the livery stable and leaving the albino in the wrangler's care, returned to Maxim's. The bartender lounged against the bar eyeing the pianist with a jaundiced expression on his face. No more than ten customers sat dotted around the big room and the hostesses were grouped languidly around the piano.

'Rye,' said Steve bringing the bartender to life. 'Where's everybody?'

The bartender gave him a sour look.

'You sure got the gall asking,' he growled. 'It's my guess you've scared all the customers away.'

Steve shrugged his shoulders and took his time over the drink. Funny thing, he thought,

216

how some honest men were quite prepared to make profit out of rustlers and killers. Rather than breathe easy in a clean town they preferred to live amongst mayhem and gunsmoke for the percentage.

Downing the remainder of his drink he left Maxim's and called in Dulin's hotel, leaving his saddle roll in his room, then made his way to Digby's staging depot. He banged a few times on the big iron door knocker and waited fully five minutes before he heard the inner door open and footsteps sound across the office floor.

The bolts shot back and the door opened enough for Digby to look out. A lamp was lit inside the office and Steve saw the man quite plainly. His big face was lit with a welcoming smile and he chewed around his straw in a completely relaxed manner.

'Well now Sherman, what can I do for you?' he asked as though any request Steve might make would receive his prompt and interested attention.

'I'd like to palaver with Miss Myra,' Steve replied. 'I guess she's still staying with you?'

Digby nodded. 'I'll tell her but it could be she doesn't want to see you. She's been saying how she's plumb tired of the way of things on the range an' she's persuaded Claire to let her travel east with us.' There was a rueful grin on the man's face as he spoke.

'You just go in and tell her Digby. I'll only accept that if I hear Myra Dean say so herself.'

Digby kept his pleasant front going. 'Yeah,' he said. 'I guess that makes sense. Just wait there an' I'll go tell her.'

He pushed through the inner door not quite closing it behind him and Steve heard him say in a casual way that Steve Sherman was waiting to talk with Myra. When Myra's reply came Steve could tell by the strain in her voice that the words she uttered held no vestige of truth and he smiled grimly to himself.

'Tell Mister Sherman I don't want to talk with him now or ever. I'm going east and the sooner the better.'

A couple of seconds later Digby reappeared. He shrugged his broad shoulders enigmatically.

'I guess it's plumb difficult to understand women,' he remarked.

Steve nodded and turned to go, then half turning caught Digby's eye.

'You're sure lucky you sold out just when you did Digby.'

'Howso?' The words came out slowly and the man's eyes became expressionless.

'Because the stage got held up this morning and three men were murdered.'

Digby puffed out his cheeks in simulated surprise but there was a frown on his forehead as he contemplated something in Steve's remark that didn't gel. Steve put him wise.

'Nearly was four men,' he added. 'Might still be if the Doc can't save Hart.'

All Digby's composure went. There was terror on his face and he seemed to lose a foot of stature in the space of a second, but Steve affected not to notice.

'Yeah, you're plumb lucky,' Steve said again. 'I sure hope the Doc can patch Hart up enough to make him talk, then we'll know who put you outa business.'

Without another glance at Digby he pushed his way out on to the sidewalk. It was a long time before the door closed and he could picture Digby hanging on to the doorpost as he considered the effect of Hart spilling the beans. When the door finally closed Steve retraced his steps and hurried along to Doc Haydn's. The Doc was at home and in response to Steve's knock he opened the door almost immediately.

'Come on in Sherman,' he said, stepping aside to let Steve through the doorway. Steve pushed the door shut quickly and the Doc shot a surprised glance at him.

'Look Doc, things have burned up some lately. The stage got held up today and four men got killed. One of 'em was Hart and it's my opinion he was siding the men who did the job. Anyways I've let it be known that

219

Hart's not dead and I've fed the information that you're trying to bring him around enough to talk. I think he was killed by his boss to save splitting the haul too many ways and I'm betting on the boss of the outfit paying you a visit muy pronto to make sure Hart does no talking.'

Doc Haydn was pouring a couple of drinks as Steve talked. He had the sort of mind that filed away information into the right pigeonhole as it was fed to him. He handed a glass to Steve.

'That means you know who's at back of things,' he said. 'Who is it?'

Steve tossed down the drink, and taking out his pocket book extracted the chewed straw and held it to the light.

'He left this behind him after the killing,' he said simply, and Doc Haydn looked at it in astonishment.

'Digby!' he ejaculated without hesitation.

'Yeah, Digby.' Steve's eyes were cold. 'I'm telling you Doc because I want you to witness the truth. In my own time I'm gonna give Digby and his sidekicks the medicine they deserve but when my report goes in I'll want your sayso that I gunned the right men.'

Doc Haydn didn't argue. He knew Sherman to be a just man and if the lawman had decided to short-circuit the law, he was sure that somehow Sherman was right.

'I want you to wait with me where we can

see who comes here,' Steve continued. 'I reckon we won't have long to wait.'

'Come on then,' the Doc said. He led the way out through the house into the rear and along behind a couple more houses and back around on to the street. Plenty of light split the darkness further down but it was possible to keep hidden in shadow where they stood and still observe the house.

They hadn't waited more than a quarter of an hour when the staging depot door opened and two figures stepped out into the night. As they passed the last saloon the stream of window light revealed them as Digby and Munro.

The two men were lost in a patch of darkness for a while then returned into view and stopped outside Doc Haydn's house. Furtively they approached the door and while Munro knocked, Digby stood alongside the door, his arm raised. For some time they remained there then Munro pushed the door open and both men went inside.

'You were plumb right Sherman,' breathed Doc Haydn then fell silent as they traced the passage of Digby and Munro in the house by the lamp light that showed through window after window. Some time passed before the men inside convinced themselves that no one was hidden in the house and it was with relief that Steve saw them emerge and return to the staging depot.

'I guess you can go back home now Doc,' he said at length. 'Just remember what you saw.'

'You bet Sherman.' Haydn gripped his arm before heading back into the house. 'And I hope you get the slimy bustard to rights.'

Steve grinned albeit grimly at the doctor's sudden show of vehemence. Maybe Doc Haydn resented having been taken in these past years by Digby's honest front.

The grin faded from his face as he considered Myra. He knew that when she had spoken earlier, Munro's gun was sticking in her back and it was certain that she would do as she was told by Digby and Munro because they would threaten to kill him in cold blood. Presuming that he still considered Digby at any event to be friendly, she must believe that he would fall an easy victim.

Further thought convinced him she was safe for the present. If they hoped to get clean away above suspicion they could not leave a corpse behind. The simplest thing would be to ride out of Blundell together in a friendly looking bunch with Myra afraid to open her mouth for his sake.

He ate a quick meal in Dulin's and after a smoke went to his room where he removed his boots and lay down on the bed. Before he fell asleep he fixed the time in his mind that he wanted to awaken and slept completely relaxed until a couple of hours before sun-up.

Long before darkness lifted he was around town, always in a position to know what Digby was doing.

He was at the hardware store further down Main Street on the opposite side to Digby's when he saw the man emerge from the front door and glance up and down before moving around the rear to the stables.

Taking his time purchasing shells and other items he required Steve kept the place under observation. At last Digby came around to the front again driving a neat buggy with a two-horse team. Strung along behind were three saddle horses. Steve recognised them as Digby's, his daughter's and the one Myra had borrowed.

The lawman came out of the store and watched proceedings openly. Munro and Digby started bringing out items of belongings from the house, placing them inside the buggy, finally struggling out with a heavy padded chair. They secured the chair then Digby climbed into the driving seat while Munro went around the side of the depot. His horse must have been saddled up in readiness because he reappeared almost instantly astride his leggy black cayuse.

Steve's heart jumped a couple of beats as the door opened and Myra came out. Dressed simply in black riding clothes with a white open-necked shirt, she appeared more beautiful than ever to him. But he saw also the tenseness of her manner and her unnatural pallor. Claire Digby was right close to her, a fixed smile on her face. She was close enough to be holding a gun and Steve guessed she was.

The two girls climbed up beside Digby, Myra in the middle, and Munro rode up alongside. Digby looked overside to where a few early-morning loungers had gathered.

'You can help yourself to what's left, Luke,' he shouted. 'Wells Fargo's bought the building and fittings but anything else you fancy, you can have.'

The man Luke thanked him and wished him good luck, then Digby shook the reins. Steve stepped off the sidewalk and into the road. He saw Claire Digby's hand hide itself behind Myra as Digby eased the horses to a stop again and took note of how Munro got himself out of view beside the buggy.

'So you're heading out Digby?' Steve kept his face stony and looked through Myra when their eyes met briefly. He saw her catch her breath as she envisaged what her words of last night had done to him.

'Yeah, like I told you Sherman. I'm all washed up here. Mebbe back east we'll fall into a better way of making a living. Anyway the young ladies will appreciate city ways so I'm thinking I'll do my duty best by making the break now.'

'Didn't know you were much for city ways Munro,' Steve said, catching the man's unwilling eye.

'Reckon I've kicked my heels long enough Sherman,' he replied coolly enough. 'They get some mighty fine rodeos back east.'

Steve stepped out of the way.

'Well, I guess you want to get going,' he said and tried not to look at Myra's agonised expression as Digby gave him a wave and shook the reins. The lawman noticed as the carriage went past that the padded leather armchair was freshly stitched in places.

Unhurriedly Steve collected his saddle roll from Dulin's and walked to the livery stable where he saddled up the albino, then as though he had no specific chore on hand rode out of town at little more than walking pace. Only when he was clear of Blundell did he give the mare her head and she settled down into the mile-eating gait he had so often admired.

Much sooner than he expected he sighted the dust raised by the swiftly-moving cavalcade of buggy and saddle horses. Turning off the trail and using every fold and rise in the undulating terrain, he closed the distance until he could see Digby and the girls quite clearly.

He noticed as he rode from point to point that Munro was riding well ahead of the buggy, a fact that gave him considerable satisfaction. It was more than likely that Munro would keep it that way to get away from the dust.

For a couple of hours Steve kept up the game of hide and seek, keeping the buggy in view as much as the terrain would allow without revealing himself. Then when just a few miles from the humped hills that formed the long canyon where Trent had died he headed away to the west behind a ridge and called on the albino for full speed. The air sang as he thrilled to the response the mare gave. She moved at breakneck speed without any apparent effort and never checked in her stride up grade or down hill. In no time he saw the cut in the hills where Marsh had tried to make his escape and he kept right on at speed until just before the entrance. When he steered the albino into the cut he noticed that her breathing was easy and her flanks rose and fell as steadily as though she had walked all the way. Rage welled up in him again as he thought that Trent would never again enjoy riding this peerless animal.

He came on to the Blundell–El Reno trail well ahead of Digby and Munro and rode down to the place where yesterday the stage had stood with the dead men strewn around. Just below, the trail curved and Steve edged his mount beside the cliff face so that the oncoming rider and carriage would be in his sight before they could see him. He didn't have long to wait.

He permitted himself a grim smile when he made out the hoofbeats well ahead of the buggy. He wasn't too worried which way he tackled the chore but one by one was easier.

Munro burst into sight with goose pimples already covering every patch of his skin. Yesterday was still too recent a memory for him to ride through this spot without some reaction. His eyes popped and his usual expression of nonchalance dropped away from him as he hauled to a stop and looked down the barrels of the unwavering Colts Steve held.

'Unbuckle that gunbelt Munro!' Steve snapped. 'And fast, or I'll let you have both barrels right away.'

Munro's mouth shaped to say something but he knew when a man was going to shoot to kill and he checked himself. Deliberately he unclasped his belt and let it slide to the ground. The buggy was close now and Steve was in a hurry.

'Get out of the saddle. Move!' he ground out the words and Munro slid down. Before he reached the ground Steve crashed one of the Colts on the man's head and Munro went down into the dust.

Scooping up the gunbelt Steve hauled Munro's horse out of the middle of the trail, then sliding out of the saddle he dragged

Munro to the side.

Digby wasn't forcing his two-horse team any up the slight grade and the buggy came around the bend at an easy pace. Steve had replaced his guns and stood in the middle of the trail, an apologetic expression on his face. Digby boggled at the sight of him but didn't panic. Myra's face held a brief expression of hope and Steve saw Claire Digby's gunhand dig into Myra's side.

The horses came to a fidgeting halt as Digby hauled on the reins in answer to Steve's upraised hand.

'Thought we'd seen the last of you Sherman,' he said, his eyes watchful. 'What in heck have you done to Munro?'

'After you left I got to thinking and I reckoned Munro was using you as a shield,' Steve answered.

Digby cast another quick glance at Munro's unconscious form and the smile came back on his lips.

'Howso?' he asked.

'He's been wandering footloose on this range ever since these stage hold-ups started. He's never been tied with Marsh to make himself an easy dollar so I reckon he's the man I'm looking for. Towing along with you made him look kinda respectable.'

Digby chewed this over and Claire, after a quick glance at Munro, must have thought on the same lines as her father. The money meant more to her than love.

'Well, I'll be goldarned,' Digby ejaculated. 'He had me fooled.'

Steve opened up Munro's saddle bags and looked towards Digby with a slow shake of the head.

'I guess he must have stashed it some-where,' he said. 'I'll take him back to Blundell. I reckon he'll talk plenty then.'

Steve stepped aside, once again catching a look of utter hopelessness on Myra's face. Digby nodded and shook the reins to start the buggy moving. When the driving seat came alongside, Steve reached out like lightning, catching hold of Claire Digby's arm, and with a vicious pull he hauled her to the ground, grabbing the gun she held in her other hand. The buggy ground to a stop again. From where Digby sat it had looked as though Claire had fallen from her seat. Digby climbed down and hurried round to where his daughter struggled in Steve's grasp.

'All right Digby. Now we can get to the rights of things.'

'What do you mean.' The smile had gone again and a nerve twitched on the man's right temple.

'I'd have told you to start with but I just had to separate you from the girl you were keeping prisoner. You are the murdering coyote at the back of the hold-ups Digby.

I've got enough evidence even without the money that's patched up in the chair you're toting.'

Myra Dean looked overside, her face shining with relief.

'It's true Steve,' she cried. 'I saw them.'

For a split second Steve took his eyes off Digby to smile up at Myra. The lapse nearly cost him his life. Digby's hand streaked to his holster and the lawman was only the bat of an eyelid in front of him as their guns cleared leather. The explosion of Steve's gun reverberated from one canyon wall to another and when the last echo died away Digby tottered a few steps then fell face downward into the dust where yesterday his own victims had lain.

Claire Digby stopped her struggling and stared transfixed at her father's body before going forward to kneel beside him. Steve turned to face Myra who had jumped to the ground. In a moment she was close to him, clinging to him as the reaction set in.

'Oh, thank God you knew, Steve,' she whispered. 'I was so afraid you believed what they made me say.'

Steve held her tight for a moment then gently disengaged her.

'See to her Myra,' he said. 'Take her up the trail a piece. I've still got things to do.'

The girl nodded and crossed to Claire Digby and after a while led her away up trail.

Steve sat on his haunches and waited for Munro to regain consciousness. The man soon stirred and after a few attempts at focusing he stared owlishly at the Marshal. When his eyes narrowed with the return of memory, Steve nodded towards the gunbelt he had thrown just out of the man's reach.

'You can fix that on again Munro. You've come to the end of the trail. You can take your choice. Leave that gunbelt off and I tote you in to get hung.'

Kurt Munro came to terms with himself quickly. He saw Digby's body in the dust surrounded by a pool of congealing blood and reckoned that only Sherman stood between him and a fortune. He reached slowly for his gunbelt. Steve was on his feet watching him carefully.

The man's mocking sardonic expression returned as he clasped on the gunbelt but Steve wasn't going to be influenced by the appearance of coolness. He stood and said nothing, his mind full of revenge for the murders of Val Trent and the young Deputy Marshal Ellis.

Just two seconds passed before Munro moved but they seemed to stretch into all eternity. They did for Munro. His speed was exceptional, his gun draw smooth, but still it was Steve's gun that fired and Munro who stood clawing at the gaping wound in his chest before keeling over. Life left him as he hit the dust and without further ado Steve hauled the two dead men on to the buggy.

Tying the albino and Munro's mount to the saddle horses at the back of the buggy, he climbed up into the driving seat and drove up trail to where the two girls waited. Claire Digby was stony faced with shock but Myra, having heard the shot, registered relief at sight of him. With the girls beside him he drove on, giving the horses their heads.

For most of the way they travelled in silence. Between Steve and Myra there was little need for conversation. Jostled together with every bump as the buggy rocked and swayed over the uneven trail, their happiness bubbled to the surface. Claire Digby just stared ahead, unable to visualise the future.

It was when El Reno was in sight that Steve gave his mind over to the problem of Claire Digby. He had enough evidence on her to ensure that she would pay the full penalty, but in the midst of his happiness he could not bring himself to let a woman pay the awful price. He looked across Myra to Claire, his mind made up.

'How in heck did you get mixed up in all this,' he asked.

For a long time Claire continued to stare ahead then she turned to look at him, her face devoid of artifice.

'I found out by accident that my father was at the back of the hold-ups,' she replied quietly. 'Then I guess I fell for Kurt pretty heavily and when I found he was in deep with my father, I reckoned I might as well accept what they were and go with them.' She paused and there was candour in her eyes. 'I guess the money mattered too. Kurt told me that he and my father met up in Dallas when they planned the whole thing. Kurt knew Marsh, who was running a trail herd to Topeka, and sold him the idea of taking the range over, the idea being that while Marsh raised hell, nobody would be looking anywhere else for stage robbers.'

'Yeah, that's the way I figured,' Steve replied. 'Well, when we hit town, you can take all your father's belongings, any dinero he carried that belonged to him, and hightail it with his outfit. I guess I've run right out of vengeance and I'm thinking you've stepped outside the law for the last time.'

Relief took over from disbelief in Claire Digby's face then the flood gates broke and she cried unreservedly as the buggy rolled down Main Street and drew up alongside the Wells Fargo depot.

Jeff Custer was standing outside talking to a group of men when Steve stepped down. He broke from the group and came down off the sidewalk. His eyes slid over the dead men then back to Steve.

'That's Digby,' he said, his eyebrows lifted in a question.

'Yeah, and Munro. They were responsible for the hold-ups. If you'll get that padded chair inside the depot and pull it apart I reckon you'll find all the dinero that was intended for the Nation.'

'Well, I'll be darned,' Custer shouted, his excitement mounting. 'Hey, come on down,' he yelled to the men on the sidewalk. 'Get that chair inside the depot.'

The men jumped down eagerly and between them manhandled the chair into the office. Custer followed quickly. Steve, after handing Myra down, followed more slowly.

'I'll be mighty glad if you hombres would take the corpses over to the funeral parlour,' Steve said, delaying Custer in his eagerness to cut the chair open. 'It's a mite harrowing for that girl out there with her father's body right behind her.'

At a nod from Custer, the men hurried outside. Looking through the window Steve saw Claire Digby climb down and follow the men to the funeral parlour. His arm stole around Myra's waist as Custer got busy with a knife. The money was there all right, every red cent of it. Custer turned and grasped Steve's hand in excitement.

'I guess Wells Fargo owes you plenty Sherman,' he said. 'When I pass my report on, I'll sure build up what you've done.'

Steve shrugged his remarks away and elbowed Myra into a chair. He pulled a faded poster out of a pocket and opening it out, handed it to Custer.

'You can do something for me now,' he said. 'That's a photo of the Laredo Kid. If Marsh hasn't got himself a shave then I reckon he'll pass for the Kid. I want you to place this poster beside a mirror on the inside of the gaolhouse door then give Marsh his guns and tell him he's not being held for the range troubles. I'll be outside and it's my guess he'll know what I'll be doing there.'

When Myra stood up to ask questions he added, 'The Laredo Kid gunned my brother Sam down and I'm set on evening the score. You stay here Myra.'

Custer took the poster and hurried away. In the gaolhouse he found a mirror and hooked it on a nail, then he nailed the poster alongside. When he took Marsh's guns along to the cells and unlocked the cell door, he started in surprise at the degree of likeness between Marsh and the Laredo Kid. The two days' growth of dark stubble on Marsh's face had transformed him. He threw the guns on to the bunk and jerked his head to the door.

'You can get to hell outa here Marsh,' he said. 'Nobody's gonna make any charges against you.'

Marsh stood up and buckled on his belt. He was puzzled but not inclined to ask questions. He pushed his way past Custer, out of the cell block and into the office. His eyes hit upon the poster and the mirror at the same time and he stood stock still, staring. The full significance struck him and the name Sherman suddenly struck home.

'So – brothers!' The words escaped from him slowly and he knew that outside Steve Sherman would be waiting.

The minutes ticked by while he drew on his courage then at last he threw the door open and walked out on to the sidewalk. Steve stood in the middle of the road, straddle legged.

'Laredo Kid! I'm taking you in for the murder of Sam Sherman, U.S. Marshal,' Steve called.

Marsh gave a harsh cackling laugh then went for his guns. The laugh died away in a gurgle that was lost in the staccato explosions as Steve's guns belched flame and Marsh pitched forward into the roadway. He tried to bring a gun to bear on Steve but his strength ebbed away and his arm drooped, the gun falling from his nerveless fingers.

Steve crossed to him before the watching crowd moved and kneeling down, turned the man over. He was riddled with bullets and had only seconds to live.

'Reckoned I'd done with the Laredo Kid,' he whispered. 'When the shack got burned down I was in town and the flashy dresser who'd just joined the outfit got mistaken for me. I reckoned I was in the clear.'

A couple of seconds later a shudder ran through the man's body and Steve stood up. His chore was done. He turned and walked through the crowd back towards the Wells Fargo depot. Myra met him halfway and walked quietly beside him. When Custer came into the office he stood and fidgeted until the girl and the Marshal broke from the embrace into which they had fallen so naturally.

'Well, I guess that folds things up for you Sherman?' Custer remarked, apologetic at breaking things up.

'Nope, not quite,' replied Steve. 'I want you to be personally responsible for seeing Miss Myra safely back to the Lazy Y. When the rest of Marsh's gang run that herd into Topeka I'm gonna be there, and with enough military to see I get what I want, and that's enough dinero to start up the folk Marsh robbed on this range.' He turned to Myra as she started in to say something. 'You just tell Ruth Pownall that there'll be money enough for Dave to start another herd. And tell her that I'd like it fine if we could get wed at the Lazy Y.'

Myra was starry-eyed as she nodded. Steve took up his hat.

'I'll use Trent's albino,' he said. 'Mebbe you'll ride my pinto when you head outa El Reno.'

She nodded again and with Custer beside her at the window, she watched the Marshal swing into the saddle of the big albino and head south on the long haul to Topeka.

The publishers hope that this book has given you enjoyable reading. Large Print Books are especially designed to be as easy to see and hold as possible. If you wish a complete list of our books please ask at your local library or write directly to:

Dales Large Print Books
Magna House, Long Preston,
Skipton, North Yorkshire.
BD23 4ND